MORE BAD
HOUSEKEEPING

MORE BAD HOUSEKEEPING

Sue Limb

Illustrations by Marie-Hélène Jeeves

FOURTH ESTATE · *London*

First published in Great Britain in 1992 by
Fourth Estate Limited
289 Westbourne Grove
London W11 2QA

First published in paperback in 1993

Reprinted 1994

Copyright © 1992 by Sue Limb

The right of Sue Limb to be identified as author of this work
has been asserted by her in accordance with the Copyright,
Designs and Patent Act 1988.

A catalogue record for this book is available
from the British Library

ISBN 1 85702 151 7

Typeset in Bembo by York House Typographic, Hanwell, London
Printed and bound by Cox & Wyman Ltd, Reading, Berkshire

one

PROMISE SPOUSE TO THINK about going to U.S.A. though infinitely more inclined to think about staying at home. Agree not to involve children in decision-making process as they will introduce non sequiturs such as Disneyland.

During next discussion with Spouse, have impression we are involved in delicate balletic manoeuvre in which we both pretend that what we really want is to be together in Winnesota, but that a malicious conjunction of tiresome external phenomena will contrive to keep us apart.

'I don't know what we could do about the house,' ponders Spouse. 'I suppose we could let it – though God knows what disasters that might lead to.'

'Elaine across the road told me they let their house once and when they came back, there was dogshit on the Axminster.'

Spouse winces fastidiously, partly at anecdote, partly at the thought of spending a year in Winnesota alongside a woman given to repeating such anecdotes. We agree on likelihood of even quiet female librarians turning into furniture-hurling, carpet-fouling, ceiling-staining viragos faced with the provocations of our innocent house.

'And then there's the car.'

We both frown convincingly at the thought of the outrages that could befall our venerable Volvo in our absence. Suspect that owners of lovable Morris Minors leave them at kindly caring kennels when they go abroad.

Lament, for first time in life, lack of pet, as necessity of abandoning furry dependant particularly harrowing. Recall dog resembling George Eliot who used to haunt our garden some time ago and which children urged me, unsuccessfully, to adopt.

'And then there's the children's education,' says Spouse, rather cleverly ignoring the paradox that it is to adorn the U.S.

Education system that he is crossing the Atlantic in the first place.

We sigh in unison at what we pretend is the cornerstone of the American approach to acquiring knowledge: all Human Experience being reduced to the Multi-Choice Question. E.g.:

Q.1: Which of these works of lidderature flowed from the immortal pen of that wunnerful liddle lady, Miss Jane Austen?
   a) Sense 'n' Sensibility.
   b) Amos 'n' Andy.
   c) Cream Cheese 'n' Gherkins (on Rye to Go).

Refrain from recalling oft-lamented destruction of British Education system by Old Smoothiechops, and instead share hallucination of Henry's and Harriet's Great British Schooldays spent composing Petrarchan sonnets, illuminating manuscripts, and performing exquisite and life-enhancing Highland Reels.

We fall silent, sensing we are now in danger of scraping the barrel *vis-à-vis* tiresome external phenomena.

'And there's no N.H.S. over there, either,' I murmur, not terribly convincing.

'Nor here either,' snarls Spouse, out of habit – but rapidly recovers and agrees that it would be just like Henry to bankrupt us with boils on arrival in what is frivolously – in medical circles at least – known as The Land of the Free.

A tremulous but promising silence falls, in which we grope our way towards consensus. A bit like a Green Party Conference session if what Alice says is anything to go by.

'Do you think you could manage the kids on your own for a year?' enquires Spouse.

Heroically refrain from observing that I have been doing just that every year since they were born, and instead demurely suppose I can but try.

'Well,' concludes Spouse, just managing to fight off expression of delirious relief, 'it's a shame, but I think it'll be a lot easier all round if you don't mind staying here.'

Assure him, with stoic dignity, that I do not mind in the least. Manage even at this moment not to think about how much easier it will be, in Spouse's absence, to have my unreliable old pipework seen to by enthusiastic young artisan.

Bask, for rest of evening, in rare glow of matrimonial concord.

two

HAVE REACHED HALF-TERM already and still not tracked down gingham school frock for Harriet. No gingham in entire town of Rusbridge. How very different from own childhood, spent swathed in checks both literal and moral.

'I blame Tesco's, or was it Asda's?' ruminates proprietor of old-fashioned Gents' and schools' outfitters in remote back street. 'Couple of years ago, they 'ad fahsands of the fings, made in Taiwan or summat, flooded the market, so yr small business said, *Right, that's it, can't compete*, and now you can't get none for love nor money.'

Trip to Cheltenham clearly becoming necessary if I am to corner last shreds of gingham in kingdom. Persuade Spouse to corral children in garden for afternoon whilst I boldly go. He agrees with a slightly better grace than usual, no doubt bearing in mind the long and painful absence from his brood awaiting him in October. Or perhaps even September if he can swing it.

Harriet clings to the hem of my garment and orders me to return with something called a Sindy Princess. Henry asks why he can't sleep out in the garden in a tent since Julian's allowed to. Instruct children to refer all requests to Daddy (asleep under *The Independent* in deckchair, and no wonder). Depart with delicious sense of freedom.

Halfway across country, realise that when Spouse is in U.S.A. for the year, I shall not be able to boldly go to

Cheltenham in search of gingham or anything else without first making extensive or expensive child-minding arrangements. Unless I bury them up to their necks in the garden for the afternoon, like play by Beckett. Wonder if Tom would happily take charge for four hours. Suspect he would make excuse about defective cistern somewhere, and depart. We shall see.

Have put myself in training and placed myself on special Single Parent High Vitamin Diet: fizzy Vit.C., Vit. B6, Evening Primrose Oil, Royal Jelly, Beta-Carotene, Brewer's Yeast, Feverfew and Bryonia 6. So should, I hope, be safe from migraine, breast cancer, P.M.T., M.S.E., Nervy and Scurvy. Wonder if it was such a good idea to take so many pills in one fell handful just before I left, washed down with half a pint of newly-opened, high-explosive Perrier.

On way down past pub, appropriately named Air Balloon, emit sudden violent Feverfew-flavoured burp, though uneasiness persists.

In Cheltenham am obliged to take car up steep helter-skelter access to parking. Have panic attack as usual halfway up. Dread misjudging lock, Volvo getting jammed, and having to be winched back into correct alignment by horde of amused and patronising men. Feel very queer even when top reached, parking space found, and concrete pillar avoided by hair's breadth.

Award myself Earl Grey and teacake, and get stuck into brilliant new novel by Anne Fine. Suspect Anne Fine may be anagram of Irish underground group. Suspect Elizabeth von Arnim may be anagram of Moslem fundamentalist group. Am idling over anagram of Pot of Earl Grey when realise that afternoon is getting on and gingham as yet unsighted.

Distracted as usual by Body Shop. Linger over Juniper and Parsnip massage oil. Wonder if year of single blessedness will include being massaged by young plumber, or whether, as I suspect, massage only occurs in pulp fiction. Buy large number of Body Shop products but only doing my bit for the planet, so no need for guilt.

4

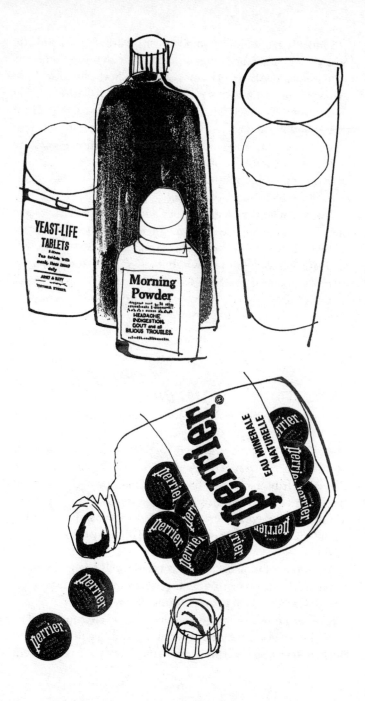

Suddenly realise it is 5.30 p.m., shops are closing, and still no sign of gingham. Never mind. Don't suppose there was any anyway. Blame Aztecs. On way home, realise have managed for some weeks now not to think about re-writing Bonkbuster. Wonder what happened to copy I flung out of train window. Even at the time, knew perfectly well that whole document was safely stored on floppy disc, so gesture entirely rhetorical. Fear my predilection for dramatic gestures may, in some final catastrophe, triumph over my bourgeois cowardice. Half-hope so anyway.

Wonder whether to give Aloes and Lavender After Shave Soothing Gel to Spouse or Tom. Then decide to do the decent thing and keep it myself. One good thing about Spouse: unaware I have returned without gingham. Indeed has no memory of, and even less interest in, purpose of my journey.

Am obliged to kill large wasp with rolled-up copy of *Resurgence*. Hope not inappropriate.

three

LIFE CLASS TONIGHT I.E. two torrid hours in Tom's attic. Tom has been strangely elusive recently so last two Life Classes have been replaced by series of gnomic phone calls and ardent cards. Have not had chance yet to tell him of Spouse's trip to U.S.A. next academic year. Perhaps when faced with a whole year of terrifying opportunity, Tom may turn back into a frog.

Afternoon of unusual peace, as Harriet and Henry are to be conveyed by another parent directly from school to Julian's birthday party which is to be Within Tent.

Have promised Superego that this echoing afternoon will be packed with domestic and professional toil. I will purchase a chicken Raised in Total Freedom in the Forests of France. I will repot and put out my *Datura Suaveolens* (a present from Alice and Saskia – and has been dangling limply in the bathroom all winter). I will also make initial heroic attempt to re-write Bonkbuster.

First succumb to strange tidal wave of fatigue. Crawl into bed and all goes dark. Suddenly I am bosom chum of Charles and Di who are living in seedy flat above shop in Peckham. Charles, depressed, confesses he was rather hurt by *Guardian*'s sneering review of his recent TV prog. Assure him I was both touched and stirred by his insights, and would be the first to stride out with him along the Shore of Solving It Together.

Recall *Guardian*'s tasteless preoccupation with disappearing royal hair, instead of disappearing rainforests, wetlands, etc. Ashamed that I have so oft sniggered at the elegant cruelties of Nancy Banks-Smith and will try harder not to in future.

Awoken by phone call from Aunt Elspeth. Have I heard the cuckoo yet? Feel this is one more domestic duty neglected. Admit not. She says portentously I'd better get a move on as it is almost too late. Open window, but can only hear signature tune of *Neighbours*. (Cornerstone of Mr Twill-next-door's post-coronary therapy.)

Feel exhausted by efforts needed to reassure Prince Charles, and to admire Aunt Elspeth's powers of ornithological organisation. Must have bath before going out to buy chicken Raised in Total Freedom, etc. Remove *Datura* from bath (where had placed it last night in vain effort to cheer it up), sluice out bits of compost and run hot water liberally laced with Body Shop Tropical Gel.

Slide therein and, in theory, plan re-write of Bonkbuster. Stare at ceiling and wonder whether Tom will cancel tonight's Life Class too – whether, in short, he is coming to his senses at long last. Unable to shed tear. Fear I am drying out, like that Russian lake, and will eventually become Pillar or rather low, indistinct mound, of salt. Sigh, and wish that I, too, had been raised in total freedom in the forests of France. It's a bit much when one begins to envy the lifestyle of a Tesco chicken.

Eventually get out, and clean bath. Rip up anti-slip rubber

mat and – horrors! – find drowned worm trapped beneath, rash emigré one assumes from *Datura* pot. Whole delicious experience of bath ruined. How very Judaeo–Christian. A worm i'th'bath. O worm thou art sick. Evidently, though Body Shop does not test its products on animals, Fate will find a way.

Using loofah, fling worm down lavatory singing brief extract from Mozart's *Requiem*. Feel sick. Too late to go shopping now. Free-range chicken a rip–off anyway. Unscrupulous marketing technique designed to exploit nostalgic longing for gîtes of yesteryear. And anyway I have planned re-write of Bonkbuster in the bath so afternoon not entirely wasted. The *Datura* can wait another day.

Descend and search for food. Can only find ancient half-empty bottle of vinegar. Hold it up to the light and observe small creatures swimming cheerfully about in it. Recoil, but then wonder: perhaps this augments rather than diminishes its capacity to nourish?

'Fish and chips again, eh?' observes Spouse acidly. Pass him the vinegar in case he needs refuelling.

On way to Tom's, wonder if it will be my fate to thrive in acidic mixture or drown in the sweet, hot unguents of the Bath of Bliss.

four

CANNOT HELP NOTICING THAT when I arrive at Porritt Gardens these days, Tom first offers me cup of Earl Grey instead of bundling me upstairs straight away. Is this the Beginning of the End? Or refinement of desire: erotic delay? Am I getting too old for all this? Is *he* getting too old for all this?

Still adorable, though, especially the way he runs his fingers through his thick, curly mane, leans back and smiles at me with his head cocked on one side. My diaphragm informs me I am still in love. Just hope to heaven he still is. Will soon find out. Announcement about Spouse's trip to U.S.A. imminent.

'Guess what – he's going to America for the next academic year.'

'*What*?!'

Disorderly flock of emotions dashes about on Tom's face: astonishment, embarrassment, delight and – unless I am much mistaken – dismay. But then pleasure bounds up like a well trained sheepdog, and crouches reassuringly on his lips, keeping everything else cowering out of sight. He seizes both my hands.

'When's he leaving? I'll move in right away.'

My turn to fight off sudden rush of alarm which flies across my features like a lime-green blush. Mumble something about taking things easy, lots of time, mustn't confuse the children, et cetera.

Tom, perhaps fanned into ardent blaze by this hint of chilly repulsion, bestows long and dizzying kiss, at which, naturally enough, phone rings. We hesitate. Tom looks guiltily past me and says the trouble is, it might be work. *Of course*, say I with probably unattractive sigh, *carry on*. Wash cups, radiating invisible pique, whilst he is on phone.

It transpires he has left his bag at the place where he was working today, complete with wallet, diary, etc., and they wish him to collect it immediately as they are about to go on holiday to Prague. Feel rather irritated by Tom's inability to organise himself, and his clients' lack of generosity in not leaving Rusbridge for Prague via Porritt Gardens, to drop off obliging young plumber's bag.

Tom bestows guilty peck, assures me he will only be half an hour, and rushes off. House very still. Suddenly notice his address book on table but am saved from burning ordeal of perusing it, by doorbell.

Girl of astounding pulchritude stands there – looks like Bellini Madonna – and enquires if Tom is in. Somehow my answer manages to suggest that he will be gone for hours and there is no point whatever in her staying. Although if she stayed, could discreetly interrogate her *vis-à-vis* nature of her relationship to him.

'Oh, it's all right,' she says, 'I'll come by another time – I just wanted to talk to him about this holiday in Tuscany we're planning.' And she goes – like a dark, velvet assassin into the night, leaving my heart in pieces on the doorstep, parts of it still pulsating faintly all over his lobelia. (NB *Must* rewrite Bonkbuster.)

Tom's walls have suddenly become blank screen upon which are projected series of extracts from blue movie entitled *Last Tango in Poggibonsi*. Sudden, panicky desire to flee, leaving enigmatic vacuum and, one hopes, disconcerting him thereby. Halfway home remember that Life Class not due to end for another hour, so spend grisly hour in the King's Arms staring into cloudy depths of glass of ginger beer. Heart as heavy as Le Creuset pan, i.e. would need industrial crane to lift it.

Whilst parking – even more eccentrically than usual – in Cranford Gardens, reflect grimly that these hot irons of jealousy do at least prove that I am Still in Love. If indeed that is a state to which any rational person would aspire.

As I let myself in, the phone rings. Answer it and am greeted effervescently by Sally. Wonder for split second who the hell Sally is, then recall remote colleague of Spouse's, stigmatised by him as infuriating woman, and once source of a few tremors on my part – not so much hot irons as tepid asparagus spears. She enquires whether she may speak with him.

'It's not urgent,' she says, 'it's just that I want to talk to him about this year in America we're doing.'

five

'GOT A MEETING IN London tomorrow,' sighs Spouse. Wonder, but do not ask, if it involves the recently resuscitated

Sally, with whom, it seems, he is to while away the academic year in Winnesota. If I could write the screenplay for this *annus mirabilis*, what would it include? A meeting of minds over waffles'n'maple syrup in a cute little emporium called *Just Desserts*, after a stimulating seventeenth century paper?

'Your analysis of the Muggletonians was so seminal –' breathes Sally –

Interrupted in middle of my first screen epic by strange stare Spouse is directing at my lower limbs.

'What's happened to your legs?' Inspect them with urgency, as Spouse's expression suggests they may have been replaced by pram wheels à la Saucy Nancy. 'Why so hirsute?' Am dumb. Have not shaved my legs for several weeks: since Tom tenderly enquired 'Why So Prickly?' Have to admit that legs now have rabbinical air. 'Somehow one associates that sort of thing with Poland,' observes Spouse, strolling languidly towards door. 'Pre-Solidarity Poland, in particular.' And with a strange, infuriating, half-amused shrug, he is gone.

Contemplate, with some dissatisfaction, my Hair Apparent. Feel it would be tactful of what is sometimes known as 'surplus hair' to go grey first, but alas! Reverse is the case. Recall all too clearly recent exclamation by Tom: 'Oh look! You're getting some grey hairs!'

Curse revealing brilliance of midsummer sun. Also curse Tom's callow, not to say callous, outburst. Had assumed he had noticed grey hairs months ago, and found them natural and right. Recall, when young, discussing how Natural and Right ageing process was, and how contemptible attempts to put back clock with Grecian 2000, etc.

Next morning, run to Boots. Whilst Spouse is in London, will perform secret trichological rituals. Purchase cream designed to Cover All Grey with Conker Brown, and another cream to bleach legs, already conker brown, a tasteful shade of blonde. Hurry children to bed and ignore Harriet's complaints that she does not feel well. Blame her choice of bedtime story: *The Slimy Book*.

When silence falls at last, unpack mystic creams. Both urge

me to test product on small area twenty-four hours before going the whole hog. Sod that. Have bit between teeth, now: squirt gravy-like substance over scalp and secure with plastic bag, then coat legs with bleach cream. Switch on 9 O'Clock News and sit back to wait statutory twenty minutes.

'Mummeee!'

Cannot move: legs are immobilised over white towel in case blobs of cream fall off and ruin carpet. (Clever, eh?)

'I'll come in ten minutes! I'm doing something!'

Then phone rings. Could be Tom. Leap to answer it.

'Can you talk? Listen, why did you piss off the other day?'

Not right moment for in-depth relationship refurbishment. Cannot properly concentrate as I have just noticed that, in my panicky sprint to phone, have scattered little white snowflakes of bleach-cream all over Spouse's ancestral Afghan rug.

'Look – I'm – I'm not quite –'

'Not quite what?'

'MUMMMeee!'

'Wait a minute! – The children aren't asleep yet.'

'Are you O.K.? Is something wrong?'

Something *is* wrong. Legs are beginning to sting. Furiously. God help the animals this stuff was tested on.

'I've got a bit of a headache actually – Ow! Ow! Ow!'

'People with headaches don't say Ow. What's going on?'

'MUMMEEEEE! Who are you talking to?'

'Nobody! – Look I'll ring you back – I've just spilt something on the carpet.'

'I'm coming round.'

'No! Don't! I'm not – not – not in the mood!'

Slam phone down.

'MummEEEE! I feel sick!'

Run upstairs, scattering bleach cream all the way on conker brown stair carpet. Cannot quite get Harriet to the bathroom in time so she is sick on my legs. Quite soothing, actually.

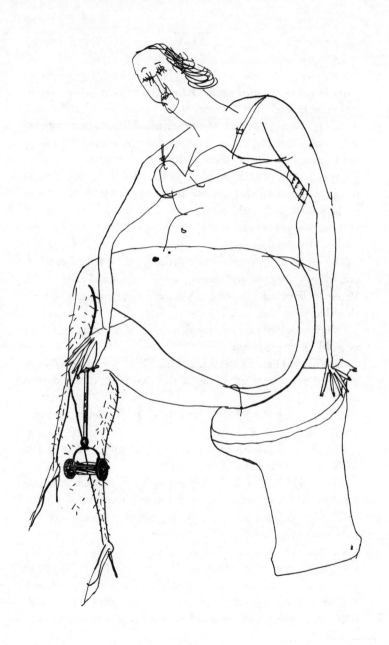

six

TOM REVEALS ON PHONE that he is off to Tuscany tomorrow. Jealously remark that Tuscany is no longer considered smart. Tom says nor is adultery but never mind, how about one for the road? Consumed with curiosity about whom he will be committing Tuscany with. Must not mention recently-glimpsed dark Venus who declared herself of the Tuscan party. Attempt to seal lips but they burst asunder like cheap garbage bag, and spill beans.

'Who are you going with?'

'Oh, the usual gang.'

The usual gang frolic in my imagination on the beach, as relentlessly elegant and young as a Next catalogue. Dark Venus is wearing jade-and-sapphire sarong upon which no child has ever been sick.

Italian beach obliterated by slamming of cosmic front door as children arrive home.

'Mummy! Henry kicked me! Can I have a gherkin? There was bird poo on the car window and Daddy wouldn't wipe it off!'

'Can we go to Legoland this year?' enquires Henry. 'Julian's going! Please please please!'

Replace phone with tender and cryptic monosyllable, and ask where is Legoland.

'Denmark,' says Spouse, depositing Tesco carrier on work-top with fastidious sigh. 'Where the strip-joints open at 7 a.m.'

Wonder, as I unpack Tesco carrier, whether Spouse's familiarity with strip-joints purely academic.

Cannot understand why unpacking shopping makes me want to scream with boredom. Would rather trundle round Tesco's for two hours than unpack it all in comfort of own kitchen for two minutes. Wonder if strippers feel similar reluctance to fish out same old unappetising wares time after time.

And yet – the anticipation of that object of desire, that hidden mystery, that –

'O Asparagus!' A cry of pure surprise and pleasure escapes my lips – the first Spouse has provoked for several years.

'*Can a Man Be Good and Sexy?*' ponders Spouse, detained by pile of old newspapers. Tempted to observe that I would be more than delighted with either and would not dream of expecting both. 'I can never quite escape the feeling,' observes Spouse, fossicking amongst ancient *Guardians* and *Independents*, 'that there's something absolutely mind-boggling hidden away in this lot.' Hoping for a *Sunday Sport*, perhaps.

'Daddy bought us Bar-b-Q Flavour Crunchblasters!' cries Harriet, seizing what used in Old Testament times to be called a crisps packet. 'It says there's a surprise in every packet!' Phone rings.

'Air Hellair Dulcie this is Sally. Could I have a word with Himself?'

'Sally wishes to speak to Himself . . . ?'

'Tell her he's out,' growls Spouse. Wonder if she was meant to hear that, and if so, whether it might be a significant factor in the Bad Men are Sexy and Good Men Not scenario. Thrust receiver at him and attend to asparagus.

Deeply grateful to learn recently that asparagus can be laid on their sides and poached and all that tedious nonsense about trussing it and standing it upright is unnecessary ritual for enslavement of women. No doubt devised by phallocentric gastrognome.

'Mummy! There isn't a surprise in my Crunchblasters!' Harriet bursts into tears. Offer her consolation prize: she may go through my jewel box. Realise too late my cache of billets-doux from Tom is therein, which could prove more of a surprise than anything Crunchblasters could secrete. Spouse replaces phone.

'You may well ask how I can have been so stupid as to ask them to lunch next Sunday,' shrugs Spouse, 'but some-how it seemed unavoidable. They're on their way to some

Godforsaken festival. My deepest apologies. I shall, of course, Help.'

New Man would simply assume he'd cook the lot, not make Gothic concession to do something manly, e.g. carve or pour (i.e. violence or sex). Never mind. Horror at necessity of entertaining entirely offset by titillation at long-postponed revelation of the mysterious Sally.

'Mummy!' Harriet rushes in bleeding. 'I've pricked myself on your *Mummies for Peace* badge!'

seven

SALLY AND LEONARD TO Sunday lunch. Agonise for hours over menu. Mad beef? Radioactive lamb? Rubber duck, high in cholesterol? Cannot face pork ever since I read somewhere it tastes closest to human flesh. Sigh. Looks like chicken raised in total freedom, etc. – again.

Although why not something foreign? More room for error when cooking something exotic, like performing avant-garde music or cutting curly hair. Consult long-forgotten Hungarian cookbook which has lain beneath piano for five years. Find recipe for Calf's Head Vinaigrette which begins: 'Remove the brain'. Hastily turn page and am confronted with 'Fried Midget Pies'. Decide Hungarian cookbook best employed as doorstop.

Spouse says Beef, of course, preferably spattered with spinal fluid. Wonder what sort of chap Spouse would be if one removed *his* brain. Mentally endow Spouse with tattoo, H.G.V. licence, chewing gum and brainless leer. Vast improvement. Have sudden flash of inspiration: salmon cutlets. But then, salmonella. . . .

Not sure what to wear, except essential to cover fat, white arms and fat, white legs. Hard to believe that handsome young Tom, e'en now frolicking with bronzed nymphs in Tuscany, actually loves me.

Decide to wear turquoise boiler suit as it covers almost everything. 'You look like an Equal Opportunities token female plumber,' says Spouse. Blush foolishly at word *plumber* and try to remember when Spouse last made observation about my appearance that was not subversive in tone.

Had assumed Sally would be tall, fair and loose-limbed but she is short and pneumatic. Had assumed Leonard was vulpine but bovine nearer the mark. Goggly eyes and faintly goitrous appearance like Kneller portrait. No wonder Sally inclines to Spouse. She adopts a bold and flirtatious manner towards him, at which demi-foolish smile plays o'er Spouse's erstwhile saturnine countenance.

Children run in and demand sweeties like she brought last time (alleged editorial visit whilst I was away in Paris). Sally produces vast bag of sweets shaped like bears, lions, pterodactyls, etc. Watch children devouring animal kingdom with Goyaesque ferocity. Leonard asks me what I think of the B1042. Wonder for a second if this is some antique manuscript but realise he is a roads buff.

Spouse locked in playful banter with Sally so I decide to carve. Difficult to do especially whilst trying to observe whether Spouse is looking at Sally's cleavage. Leonard delivers panegyric on the M40, and I pretend to listen whilst telling Harriet for the sixth time to wash her hands. When I finally enquire of Spouse, 'Breast or leg?' it is with a strange louche emphasis. Hope no-one notices.

Also hope no-one notices that I put salt in the carrots twice. They appear to have been marinated in the Dead Sea. Leonard asks me what is the best place to park in Bath. Suddenly have apocalyptic, and possibly premonitory, glimpse of Spouse and Sally in bath together discussing Love Sex and Marriage in the seventeenth century.

Leonard enquires which is the best, the A34 or the B1432. Cannot reply as am possessed with speculation about whether Sally is 42C or 40D. Brief downward glance confirms that own bosom has mysteriously disappeared. Feel I am coming to resemble cheap duvet in which most of the kapok has sunk to the bottom.

'Summer pudding?' I enquire with casual élan, at which Sally bounces with enthusiasm and Leonard cries, 'Summer pudding and 'B' roads! You have a place in my heart forever!' Smile gratefully, though would not be seen dead in Leonard's heart. Suspect it has not passed its M.O.T.

Ladle out summer pudding airily, for all the world as if I had not sworn blue murder several times during its manufacture.

'Mummy?' says Henry as we all savour exquisite mélange of berries, 'Why does dog poo go white once it's been lying about for a while?'

'I don't like this, it's sour!' yells Harriet, and returns to her bag of endangered species.

Under the pressure of summer pudding, another button on Sally's corsage comes undone. Leonard confides, winking, he is not going to the States as the roads are too straight and he and I will have to get together in our grass widowhood, won't we? Heart sinks several hundred fathoms. Will need the engineering genius of a Red Adair to get it up again.

eight

ACHING VOID IN NATURE left by World Cup, Wimbledon, etc., filled by Rusbridge Primary Sports Day. Cannot resist enquiring if I may look forward to Spouse's company. He goes pale and says Not this year dear I've got a headache.

Surrender to martyred sigh. Own enjoyment of sports limited to Brian Johnson's cake commentaries.

Postman brings parcel from Aunt Elspeth: real Panama Hat in its own balsa wood travelling box, designed to protect Spouse's sacred brain from the worst of the Winnesota sun.

'Can't think why she's sent it,' he remarks. 'Unless she's forgotten that she's supposed to be coming here for the last week of August.' We both feel this is too much to hope for, and shudder in unison at the thought of her advent. In fact the only time we do shudder in unison, these days, is at the thought of Aunt Elspeth. Perhaps she will save our marriage.

Hat very elegant, though, and Spouse lends it me for Sports Day. Join other Class One mums on rickety bench in windswept school field. Enquire of undernourished-looking mother of Gabrielle where she is going on holiday this year. She observes with asperity Day Trip to Weymouth if she's lucky. Aghast at my lack of social tact, avert my eyes.

Behold Harriet corralled with classmates short distance away. Harriet mouthing urgent messages to me: TAKE THAT HAT OFF. Ignore this. Rather pleased with hat. It makes me look like a short, fat, snub-nosed, talentless version of Virginia Woolf – which, let's face it, is as near as I'm going to get.

Harriet comes fifth in her race and bursts into tears. Observe to Gabrielle's mum that I'm not sure competition is such a very good thing. She replies that her mum won a food processor once and it was nothing but trouble.

Mums' Egg and Spoon race looms and we are cornered on our bench by Headmistress in no mood to be denied.

'Come along Mrs Domum! You've got your sensible shoes on – there's no excuse!'

Recognise, with qualm, Prime Ministerial tones and am instantly transformed to quivering blancmange – a sort of Cabinet Pudding. Slink to starting line, along with Gabrielle's mum in stilettoes. Obscurely annoyed that Headmistress should refer to my Eccos as sensible shoes, even though that is what they are.

Small, bald man – presumably parent unable to produce

headache – lines us up and cries: 'MARX GETS – a – GO!' Evidently out of tune with the times.

We lurch forward. After twenty paces, somehow my right Ecco catches on my left Ecco and I crash to the ground, in tropical billows of Monsoon skirt, perhaps even revealing a matronly flash of Sloggi maxis. Not so much Egg on Spoon as Egg on Face.

Get up and complete race with sporting smile stapled to face to hide deep sense of ignominy and stinging palms. Gabrielle's mum has triumphed on her high heels and is solicitous towards me. Assure her I am fine, not hurt at all, never felt better, did it on purpose actually, nothing like a pratfall to make a party go with a swing. Secretly convinced I have cracked ribs and that stomach has been twisted off its stalk, dislodged and flung into groin.

Dare not look at Harriet as convinced that my making such a spectacle of myself will cause her long-term psychological damage.

Offered cup of tea and gladly withdraw to school hall where group of grans have set up a Day Care centre for bruised competitors.

'You've got blood on your chin, dear,' says someone I believe to be an Emily's Gran. Retire, alarmed, to Girls' Toilet and behold my mirror image bearded with mud and blood. Wash face, and blot wound on skirt, in customary absence of handkerchiefs, soft loo paper, etc. Patterned skirts essential once parenthood sets in.

Reunited with Harriet who sobs inconsolably, apparently because I was not only prone but also last.

Feel that Sports Day underlines essential brutality of Darwinian struggle and that Eastern Europe should think hard before surrendering to full blown market economy. Decide however not to confide this thought to Emily's Gran, who says it's been a wonderful day hasn't it. Agree. Whilst driving home, pray that Spouse has not finished off the last of the Paracetamol.

nine

Spouse takes Henry off to East Anglian Air display. They are to stay the night at Leonard and Sally's weekend cottage in Norfolk. No doubt cottage will eventually be burnt down by Norfolk Nationalist Movement (a.k.a. The Flat Earth Society). Wonder if Sally will pack Leonard and Henry off to explore the 'B' roads around Walsingham leaving her and Spouse 'Alleyne togetha at lawst!' in a glorious vista of ripening wheat and knapped flint.

Pleasant to have double bed to myself. Anticipate relaxed day tomorrow with my darling daughter. Dream, at last, of Gordon Brown, he of the strangely magnetic lips, Byronic hair and fiscal genius. We are in a private compartment on a romantic night sleeper rattling through Europe. 'Do explain the E.M.S. to me, Gordon!' I beg. 'Firrst, my dear Dulcie,' murmurs the great man, 'let us drraw the blinds. . . .'

'Mummeee! Had a bad dreeeem!'

Gordon Brown spins away from me in a thousand wheeling fragments, and vanishes with a pop. No doubt John Major would welcome the same sensation.

Harriet leaps into bed on top of me, her knees burying themselves accurately in my tender premenstrual bosom like a pair of heat-seeking missiles.

'Had a *dream*. . . . I was being chased by a giant man-eating kangaroo. . . . Horrible . . . fright'nin'!'

Alarm clock informs me it is 6.15 a.m. Comfort Harriet and urge her to fall asleep again and have a nice dream instead. But no. Useless.

'I'm *hungry* Mummy!'

'Well go down to the kitchen and get yourself a banana.'

'No! Frightened! *Witches* down there. . . .'

Lurch from bed in manner of badly bandaged mummy from Hammer films, select banana, and install Harriet before TV with video of *The Lion, the Witch and the Wardrobe*: Christian parable in which Lion is mocked and killed but rises again, shakes his majestic mane, and leads the Good to victory in the Battle. Cannot resist shedding tears of pious exhilaration whenever I watch it, even though all other symptoms of Christian education have long since disappeared. Mind you, in premenstrual mode, have been known to weep in pious exhilaration at baked bean adverts.

Return to bed hoping for extra doze. Also hope Harriet will not switch off video and tune in to some early morning aberration: striptease from Denmark, perhaps. Labour may have promised nursery education, but my vote will go to Party guaranteeing ideologically sound, educational, entertaining children's TV programmes from 5 a.m. daily.

Drift into shallow slumber but Gordon Brown has been replaced by stern woman who informs me that in ten minutes I have to take my English 'A' level exam. Realise with horror I have forgotten to read any of the set books, and from this protracted nightmare Harriet resolutely neglects to rescue me.

Awake eventually with headache at 8.30. Dress, and take Harriet's clothes downstairs. Switch off TV and sit down to dress her.

'How dare you switch off the TV Mummy you horrible poo!'

'Don't you talk to me like that!'

'I hate you, you pooey bum!'

'Do you want a smack?'

Harriet punches me hard on ear. Wheel her round, whip up her nightie, and administer not-too-hard-I-hope smack on her bare bottom. To my horror, red handprint materialises on the fair flesh like some supernatural emblem of guilt. The Mark of Cain, the Turin Shroud, the Hand of Domum.

Harriet screams hysterically. Wonder how hard Di slapped William, and with all the world watching, too. My heart goes out to her. She should be President of Smack the Children Fund. Wonder if horrible handprint will eventually fade but fear it is branded on my soul for ever.

'I hate you I hate you, you horrible pooey-bonker!'

Phone rings. Seize it, and discern Tom's faraway tones across crackling Euro-distance: tired, melodramatic, and, unless I'm mistaken, drunk.

'I've been up all night . . . and you know, *thinking* and stuff . . . and I just wanted to say I love you madly, right? And I want to be with you and take care of you and sod it, I want to *give you babies* – ' Mercifully the line goes dead as Harriet sinks her teeth with Rottweilerian panache, deep into my ankle.

ten

TIME HAS COME TO confront dreaded hols. Have rented cottage near Dolgelly for a fortnight from 7th August, where Harriet and Henry can catch slugs whilst I gaze enraptured at rocks and rowans, and Spouse can do some 'proper walking'. Suspect that 'proper walking' means without children. Gazing at rocks and rowans, however, can apparently be performed simultaneously with extensive childcare, shopping and cooking. How jolly convenient that I do not also aspire to the sacred art of proper walking.

Wonder if it will rain in Dolgelly and add LEGO people, books, toys, puzzles, etc., to immense Holiday Packing list. Cottage apparently has TV, so Spouse will be immobilised in armchair if there is a Test Match against the Indians. What you might call 'proper sitting'. The quality of Test Matches seems to improve, the more intense and bloody the previous colonial struggle. Seems a shame we do not play against the I.R.A.

Looking forward to Torrent Walk, where Spouse and I canoodled fifteen years ago. In our case it was torrid walk. Perturbed recently to read that bracken can cause cancer as distinctly recall our spending several hours horizontal in it. Spouse denies all knowledge of this episode and says I must be thinking of someone else. And indeed, I usually am, these days.

Frustrating that the minute Tom returns from Tuscany, I am forced to leave Rusbridge for family holiday. Still, further separation can only add to the tingling sense that, once Spouse flies off to Winnesota, we shall have world enough and time.

Saskia sends me brochure for week in Devon under canvas: arts workshops, music, theatre, lots of wonderful things for kids to do.

'*Discover your ecological self,*' sneers Spouse, '*through Native American Medicine wheels, shamanic teachings and deep ecology.* Not bloody likely.' Reply that if ever his Ecological Self was brought to light by Native American medicine wheels, the best thing they could do would be to run over it.

Spouse dispenses scorn impartially towards Tarot, Raku and Biorhythms. Scorn is a great comfort, of course – a bit like religion, I suppose.

Am myself ravished at the thought of the Raku and the Biorhythms. Indeed, reading the brochure reduces me to tears – a bit like the Ode to Joy. Wonder if my lachrymose tendencies have developed in response to the scorching drought of Spouse's sensibility. Spouse declares sardonically that he would like nothing better than to live under canvas for a week surrounded by hordes of lefties and their Yahoo children but, alas, he must finish his article on the Levellers before Dolgelly. It is therefore agreed that Henry, Harriet and myself will go a-Rakuing without him. Must pack in a hurry though as it all starts immediately.

'You might as well get some practice in at being a single parent,' observes Spouse with a sadistic smile. Inform him that I am already so practised, could do it with my eyes shut. Uneasily aware, however, that being single parent may lead to the eyes being shut a lot less often than one would choose.

Compare and contrast Spouse of the sadistic smile with ardent Caledonian of yesteryear panting in the bracken. Not sure I've improved all that much either. But at least I've got a panting partner. Realise with flash that that is what Spouse needs, too, and that the sooner he flies off to Winnesota with Sally, the better.

But what am I saying? (Elastoplast, scissors, Sellotape . . .) Is the end in sight? Is this bolt of his across the Atlantic an escape for us both? (Bog paper, towels, Swiss Army knife . . .) And what exactly are my feelings about it?

Why is my fear of what Spouse may get up to with Sally insignificant compared to my fear of what I may get up to with Tom? (Hairbrush, camera, thermos, headache pills, hot-water bottle, National Trust Membership Card . . .)

Feel I may need the divination skills of the Native American Medicine wheels. If they work, I shall recommend them to my own favourite redmen: Neil Kinnock and Gorbachev. And there's always Dolgelly. Wonder if I should try a pounce in the bracken for old time's sake. If we can get a babysitter. . . .

eleven

AT WEST COUNTRY ARTS Camp, Henry and Harriet love storytelling round the campfire – perhaps because folk tales often dwell on ingenious mutilations. Fairy tales evidently suitable preparation for 1990s after all. Own camp experiences include consultation with Tarot reader under blasted oak. Warned of trials ahead with Emperor and Magician.

On our return, greeted by Spouse, or perhaps Emperor, in grumpy mood. Considering I had taken children out of his hair for a week, feel I might have been welcomed with smiles, cups of Earl Grey, congratulations on my tan, etc., rather than 'Is that just your rubbish in the car? I don't know how you do it.' Privately reflect that if he thought car was a mess, lucky he didn't see tent, especially on occasion when Henry first left top off, then trod on, tube of Sun Protection Factor Fifteen.

Scarcely time to open post before packing for Dolgelly. Tactfully typed envelope reveals request from Tom (a.k.a. the Magician, I assume) for my address in Wales. Confide it in snatched phone call whilst Spouse is vacuuming car with persecutory zeal hitherto only displayed by Judge Jeffreys. Long to receive romantic love letter on Celtic fringe, though not sure it would be worth risk. Tom assures me if he cannot communicate with me before September he will go mad.

At this moment Henry and Harriet rush in shouting Mummy, Mummy what's a Muslim?

'Er – somebody with a different God from ours. Theirs is called Allah.'

'Alan?'

Terminate amorous phone call in the interests of multicultural education. Alas.

Welsh cottage idyllic. Up secret wooded lane, with tiny secluded suntrap of a garden, miles from civilisation, etc. Spouse maliciously reminds me that I once declared I must always live within screaming distance at least of nearest neighbours. Retort that it's different on holiday.

On shopping trip next day, meet and converse with ancient farmer. Enquire what time the postman comes. Farmer utters bitter laugh and says It depends if it's Dewi. Not sure if *Dewi* a reference to weather conditions or a name, but offer thanks and promise will not let children near sheep. Afterwards wonder if sheep are radioactive and redouble determination on last point.

First week includes many outbursts of Proper Walking by Spouse, on grounds that he must fit it in before he crosses Atlantic as Walking is un-American activity and can lead to being shot. Eventually though he concedes that I deserve a day to myself and takes the children off to Barmouth. Sink blissfully into suntrap with old *Guardian* and bask in perfect stillness and delightful absence of family.

Read article which seems to be lamenting a decline in the quality of mass murderers. Suddenly roused from sleepy torpor by furtive footstep in lane. Eyes inform me that someone in jeans is crouching on other side of hawthorn hedge. Brain immediately concludes it is mass murderer, probably of the new low-quality type.

Sun goes in, blood freezes and legs turn to stone. In the

circumstances therefore a miracle that I manage to get up and run indoors, lock all doors and lurk, with madly beating heart, in pantry. Implore Al (short for Almighty) to prevent my murder and promise in return never again to betray Spouse, a man made in His image if ever there was one.

Minutes pass. Sun comes out. Feel this is a Sign, and am beginning to relax when hear stealthy tread on gravel immediately outside back door. Convinced I am about to die, seize breadboard as cannot bear knives even for self-defence.

Suddenly shadow of tall man flits past kitchen window. Scream, cringe, and then hear furtive voice, without:

'Is that you, Dulcie? You scared the hell out of me.' Fling open back door and behold Tom.

'Oh no! You didn't come all the way here just to see me! You idiot!' Fall into his arms.

'Don't flatter yourself, darling. I just happened to be passing.'

Subsequent five hours in remote clump of bracken more than compensates for absence of family. Aware I have broken my promise to Al, but hope he has too much else on his plate to notice.

twelve

AUNT ELSPETH COMETH. ARANS are dispensed and have to be tried on and admired in sultry heat. Mine makes me look like a walking porridge. Henry throws his off, and asks whether she has secreted in her basket a video of Teenage Mutant Turtles. Aunt Elspeth enquires if this is a wildlife film and, if so, she's all for it. We then get forty-five minutes of The Extraordinary Behaviour of House Martins this year, after which Harriet announces loudly that she can smell a fart, whose was it?

Adjourn to garden. Aunt Elspeth observes with pursed asperity that the children are more 'wonderfully high-spirited' than ever. Our garden also clearly an aberration. A.E. perceives that my astrantias are wilting but what can one expect? Not sure if this is sympathetic acknowledgement of climatic conditions or verdict on my management. A.E. also laments absence of nice bright dahlias and chrysanths. Assure her that though own garden dismal, nearby Assington Manor open to the public on Sunday and will be delighted to convey her thither.

On Sunday, confounded by sudden disappearance of car keys. Conduct search in languid manner initially to deflect suspicion but Spouse notices all too soon.

'What on earth have you lost now?'

All hands on deck: whole household ransacked but no sign of keys. Suspect, not for first time, existence of Black Hole in my study but cheerfully blame wonderfully high-spirited children who have, before now, wonderfully high-spirited away passports, Building Society passbooks, etc., to their nests.

'Rather like jackdaws,' I conclude, hoping this ornithological reference will disarm stern aunt.

'The jackdaw is an absolute menace,' confirms Aunt Elspeth grimly.

Spouse produces spare ignition key, in my view unnecessarily late and with unpleasant trump-card air. Aunt Elspeth wonders whatever I will do once he has gone to Winnesota. Tempted to inform her, but refrain.

Spouse and Henry excuse themselves from Assington Manor Garden on grounds of motorsport on TV. Personally feel that exposure to TV motorsport would qualify one for support of Amnesty International. Would prefer Henry to develop a taste for limp astrantias at no matter what cost in grandchildren. But of course Aunt Elspeth colludes in idea that one could never expect Real Men to be dragged off to a mere garden and makes jocular reference to Ladies Withdrawing. Diverted by idea of self as lady, let alone Harriet as anything more ladylike than Rottweiler.

Assington exquisite, though tea somewhat spoiled by

Harriet's picking her nose and placing the evidence on the side of my plate. Aunt Elspeth declares Harriet needs a firm hand and laments anew Spouse's U.S.A. trip. Riled by this – because though serenely reconciled to Spouse's departure, I do secretly wish he could somehow contrive to leave his firm hand behind.

Upon returning to car park discover I am boxed in by two Range Rovers. Parking is such sweet sorrow. Extricated with help of thin faced man in tweed cap – suspect Lord Ass himself. On way out of gate, notice with horrid qualm that fuel gauge has sunk to bottom of the red. Crawl in high gear to main road whence Rusbridge only fifteen miles as the crow flies – or as the house martin flies, one hundred and fifty.

Creep into forecourt of petrol station with sigh of relief. Do not care about price hike: just grateful pumps are still full. But o woe! *Where is key to petrol tank?* Still down Black Hole in study back home, that's where. Brain struggles with dilemma in vain: think-tank evidently empty too. Necessary above all to avoid being rescued by Spouse.

Get back into car and propose pause for ice creams. In historico–cultural terms, a significant moment: when the oil ran out. Should really fling ignition key over nearby hedge, breathe deeply, feel native earth beneath feet and set out joyfully on foot, ears ringing with bird song. Cannot help feeling it would be more convenient for oil to run out when Aunt Elspeth back home in Kirkwhinnie.

She confides she does not want an ice cream thank you dear, she would rather we went home as quickly as possible as she thinks she is getting one of her attacks.

thirteen

OUT OF GAS, AND petrol tank irrevocably locked as key is at home, where Spouse and Henry are watching TV motorsport.

Harriet demands ice lolly shaped like human foot. Tendency of toes to drop off and melt all over upholstery.

Sensible thing would be to ring Spouse and request he bring petrol tank key somehow, but how? Taxi, on a Sunday? Against his Caledonian good husbandry. Cringe at thought of caustic observations he would feel entitled to make. Horribly tempted to ring Tom, though goodness knows what he could do, and what would Aunt Elspeth say if he turned up instead of Spouse? Although he could wear his plumber's rig and pose as professional tank-cracker.

Give in to impulse. Tom assures me there's always more in the tank than you think and suggests I float home in highest possible gear. Advises me to buy a can of petrol to take with me. He can't really get away right now as he's got some people round and they're just sitting down to lunch. But if car actually grinds to a halt, do ring him again, no sweat. Express, though do not significantly experience, gratitude, and suppress irritation at people who sit down to Sunday lunch at 4.30 p.m. Adolescent habit, like lying in bed till noon and using expression 'no sweat'.

Inform Aunt Elspeth and Harriet that we are to crawl homewards in high gear and hope for the best. A.E. remarks that she always rises to a crisis and urges me to switch off the cassette player to save petrol. Know that without Roald Dahl's *The Witches*, Harriet would go critical after about three miles. Explain that cassette player runs off electricity and is nothing to do with petrol.

'Are you absolutely sure about that?' she barks, and I begin to doubt my own instincts. Aunt Elspeth also suggests it will use up less petrol if Harriet lies flat on the back seat and does not talk. Harriet readily agrees in spirit of wartime co-operation. Feel Aunt Elspeth may after all have a few canny ideas in her head. Ignore her advice to ring Spouse, however. Determined to get her home under my own steam, and quite prepared to push Volvo up hill if necessary.

Astonishingly, Volvo reaches bottom of Cranford Gardens before expiring with graceful sigh. Aunt Elspeth enjoys the hundred-yard stroll home as she can criticise other people's gardens. Spouse greets me affectionately: after all, I have removed his aunt from his sight for a whole afternoon. Aunt Elspeth's attack successfully intercepted by algae tablets.

'They'd stop anything, dear,' she confides menacingly. Spouse makes tea, confirming A.E.'s opinion of him as extraordinarily helpful around the house, she hopes I realise how lucky I am. Secure key to petrol tank, run down road, and administer canful of the elixir of life to parched old Volvo. Mr Twill appears and enquires whether I think it will be all over by Christmas. 'All over' has more apocalyptic ring than in 1939. Suggest he makes bunker out of one of his marrows. He laughs and says I am a marvellous gel.

Drive the hundred yards home with light heart, aware that Spouse will be next one to use car and it's his problem now. Convinced anew that our dependence on fossil fuels has led to profoundly unreasonable and reckless life-styles, e.g. visiting gardens fifteen miles away. Wonder if the drying-up of fossil fuels would have good effect on moral tone of nation. Less adultery, that's for sure.

Join family for cup of tea. Spouse has quarried immense Dundee cake brought by Aunt Elspeth and children are flicking currants at each other. Consume large slice with appreciative smile, though I cannot bear dried fruit. Aunt Elspeth remarks with tragic expression it is so sad for the dear children to lose their father for a year. Cannot help agreeing, and suggest Spouse takes them with him to U.S.A. instead.

fourteen

GREAT AUNT ELSPETH RETURNED unopened to Kirkwhinnie – which is something of a triumph given her predilection for gastro-urological disorder. She pauses on the platform of

Rusbridge Station for valedictory maledictions. Fixing Spouse with basilisk eye, she requires him to avoid all American swimming pools as they are awash with the HGV virus.

She further suggests that at the first whiff of chemical warfare he must fill his Panama hat with Scottish oatmeal, soak it with Johnnie Walker, and strap it o'er his face. Lastly, he is to find time in his frantic transatlantic schedule to pause awhile and remember with tenderness his dear little wife and bairns at home.

Spouse looks startled at this, as though detected in bigamy, but is obviously reassured by a brief glance confirming that I am in fact big and bolshie rather than dear and little. Though perchance the warped lens of sentimental retrospect will reduce me to something of a Mrs Tittlemouse, in time.

'Do your laces up, Henry,' barks Aunt E. as her train at last pulls out. Henry serenely ignores this. His new trainers are as huge, hi-tech and white as the Pompidou Centre and he wears the laces resolutely undone. They droop down in melancholy symmetry like the moustaches of a pre-revolutionary Chinese mandarin. Wonder if his undone laces represent the dawn of sartorial awareness or pre-teen death wish.

Harriet, requested to place lolly wrapper in bin, bursts into tears and declares she feels sorry for the rubbish. Recognise, with dual pangs of sympathy and foreboding, the dawn of liberalism.

Spouse's last week in Albion spent by him in crating and sending off large numbers of books. Would have thought that the Cyrus Z. Fishplucker Memorial Library could have supplied identical tomes, but Spouse explains he cannot bear to be separated from his own marginalia.

Attempt to pack his underpants without a qualm, and to imagine his frantic transatlantic lifestyle. Suspect he may find enough time on his hands to stroll through fields of rippling nymphets. Can imagine disastrous effect of his saturnine élan upon free-range, corn-fed Freshwomen.

Spouse suggests farewell lunch at aptly-named local pub

The Fleece. Warm enough to sit out and feast his eyes for last time for many months on the scorched, scorched hills of home. Henry and Harriet opt for Bangers'n'Mash but at crucial moment Harriet enquires if sausage was ever alive. On learning that it was, she screams and throws it sideways onto adjoining table where immaculate retired couple had been enjoying pastoral idyll. Retrieve sausage with craven smile of apology and hustle children home early where they can misbehave in private.

Spouse finds among his old newspapers-for-packing one with the headline GAZZA CHOKED. Suggests that if I should require a toyboy in his absence I should look no further than Mr Paul Gascoigne. Wonder why Paloma Picasso has not bottled and merchandised his tears at £150 per half ounce? Mrs Thatcher could then defy Europe with bag by Gucci, smile by Saatchi and dab of *Lacrime Gazzi* behind each ear.

Though sudden death penalty shoot-outs a mangled travesty of justice when concluding football matches, feel they would be a good way of solving international crises.

Tom rings to ask Has He Gone Yet? Snap out irritated reply and hang up. Quite prepared to consort with Tom whilst Spouse here, or indeed there, but seems somehow tasteless during period of packing and preparation.

Spouse celebrates last night in Rusbridge with attempt at amorous dalliance. Unfortunately we both fall asleep halfway through. Woken at 2.30 a.m. by vigorous birth-pangs of pun. Mr Paul Gascoigne should fall in love with Welsh girl, thus enabling tabloids to describe photo of their embrace as *Eirlys'n'Gazza*. Despite superior claims for attention of international and domestic crises (imminent loss of Spouse and unavoidable rushing-in of Tom to fill vacuum, not to mention dawn of Henry's angst and Harriet's bleeding-heart socialism): the self-important intricacy of this pun continues to fascinate subconscious mind for hours. Wish, not for first time, that my education had been concluded not at Cambridge but at Gas Street Secondary Modern.

fifteen

DREAM THAT ARTHUR SCARGILL rings me up and asks if he can bury mysterious biscuit tin in our garden. At the time feel this is somehow to do with the Holy Grail but upon awakening think perhaps not. All thoughts of King Arthur driven briskly from my mind at recollection that this is day of Spouse's departure and I must drive him to Heathrow.

Find him drinking coffee and getting his last taste of British TV News. Extract from Iraqi TV convinces me that Saddam Hussein has the eyes of an unreliable old spaniel who knows he has pooed on the carpet but is hoping to get away with it. Children rush in naked and make series of unreasonable demands about eating breakfast whilst watching TV. Spouse makes loud noise and they disappear.

Uneasily aware that Spouse's going to U.S.A. for a year is a sort of unilateral disarmament, and feel my lifelong membership of C.N.D. may have been a mistake after all.

Tracey arrives to conduct children to her Mum's for the day. She has acquired kohl black eyes, mask white cheeks, and a bunch of green dreadlocks through which she peers like last surviving panda through grove of bamboo.

Provide Spouse with Passport, U.S. currency, airline reservation, freshly-packed suitcase containing a fortnight's clean underwear, shaving tackle, his current bedside reading, etc., etc. Then drive him to Heathrow and deliver him to correct terminal. Spouse bids me farewell with final 'Good Luck', and pitying shake of head, as if doubtful whether poor disorganised Dulcie will manage to get through to the week's end, let alone the year's, without him.

Walking back to car park, feel sudden gigantic thundering in loins and anticipate for a moment Armageddon, Transfiguration, or at very least onset of epic cystitis, but it is only Concorde taking off. Am moved, against my will, by its brute grandeur and aquiline profile heading westward. Rather like Spouse in a way.

Drive home, not with anticipated sense of freedom, but gathering gloom. So many ordeals ahead. Henry and Harriet bound to celebrate removal of totalitarian tyranny by endless internecine bickering (cf. U.S.S.R., South Africa, etc.). Somehow dread Tom's inevitable arrival as feel I need space to myself for a few precious seconds first.

Worst of all, received PC this morning from Jeremy D'arcy, wondering 'how the rewrite was going'. Guiltily aware that Bonkbuster has been gathering dust all summer and that even Jeremy's fatuous editorial suggestions are forgot.

Feel somehow I have reached rock bottom and have nothing left to give maternally, erotically and above all creatively. Come over queer, pull over onto hard shoulder and burst into tears.

After five mins' snivelling, grab old paper bag off floor, smooth it out on *Road Atlas of Great Britain*, seize pen and write:

So this was the New World. Peveril St Canonicorum de las Palmas de Santa Cruz leaned his fatigued head back appreciatively against the deep upholstery of the Union Pacific Railroad. Why had he come here? Was it the shock of finding that Charlotte had run away and left him? And with Cherbagov, of all people! Not only a serf, but shorter, balder and older than Peveril himself. How could she?

Peveril's aristocratic lip quivered at the consciousness of his wife's insult. Where she and Cherbagov had fled, he knew not and cared little. But he himself had felt propelled mysteriously westwards, onwards, towards some kind of transcendent truth.

Peveril was travelling light, with nought but the old Magyar-skin ottoman given to his grandsire by the old Czar; and with only one servant. It was the youth Dmitri, whom Peveril had plucked off a dunghill. He was now dozing on the ottoman in the baggage car. As yet Dmitri had not revealed much save a sulky indolence of manner, and Peveril assumed worse would follow, but he somehow did not care.

The train's melancholy wail echoed among the infinite black velvety spaces of the savannah night, a strange exotic scent filled his nostrils, and a feeling of loneliness and sweetness possessed his soul. He was on his way.

sixteen

'Bring the carriage round again at midnight, Dmitri.' Peveril was not anticipating a long evening. At St Petersburg, years ago, he had danced till dawn. At his Betrothal Ball with Charlotte on the Eve of St Mikhail Ignatieff he had pranced till his pigskin pumps split. But this was not St Petersburg. This was Hicksville, Georgia.

Not his Georgia – or rather, Dmitri's. Dmitri hailed from Tbspsvili, had travelled north during the Mouldy Fig Famine of '88, and had appeared, a tattered figure, at the gates of Yeltsinborg that autumn.

Peveril banished the tedious intrusions of geography and history from his mind as he stepped stiffly into the glittering ballroom and concentrated, with some relief, on the exacting problem of preserving a haughty demeanour. He would show Hicksville, U.S.A., the meaning of an aristocratic mein. Or was it mien? 'I' before 'E' except after – but Peveril's education at St Gyorgy's Military Academy had not included any extensive exploration of spelling.

He scanned the ballroom with an austere stare and was, despite himself, impressed. It may only have been Hicksville, U.S.A., but all the bloom of Marlon County was there. Fifty pairs of soft enquiring eyes had marked the entrance of the stranger, fifty lovelocks tossed in agitation upon as many gleaming brows, and a hundred snowy breasts surged impetuously against the constraints of whalebone and satin stretched shrieking-tight.

The flunky cleared his throat. This was the moment he had

been waiting for all his life. This was, he decided, the moment that put Hicksville on the map.

'Peveril St Canonicorum!' he roared, 'De Las Palmas de Santa Cruz!. . . . Yes, sir!'

'Lawdy, Momma,' drawled doe-eyed Miss Donna Pershing drowsily from the fluttering petals of her orange-blossom-bedecked corsage, 'how many people is that?'

Phone rings. Spouse, sounding unnervingly close, reports safe arrival in Winnesota. He has however encountered a series of infuriating obstacles to do with his having lost his driving licence and therefore his identity. Moreover, the office, secretary, and FAX machine promised by Rick Dill have not materialised. His apartment is phoneless and will remain so for a fortnight. He is ringing from 'a colleague's' and must therefore be brief.

Suspect 'colleague' is fellow ex-pat academic Sally and enquire disingenuously as to her health. Spouse replies 'Fine', confirming my suspicions. Had it been another colleague's he would not have resisted some caustic aside. On being asked to dilate upon the beauties of Winnesota, Spouse observes it is the *Anus Mundi*, sighs a particularly martyred sigh, and hangs up.

Unable to point out that Winnesota does at least offer one attraction: absence of parental responsibility. Produce even more martyred sigh of my own. Would willingly spend a week in the Great Intestine of the World if allowed in return to wake up when I will, rather than being brutally awoken at 6.30 a.m. by requests to buy them a gerbil to make up for Daddy being away. Attempt to discover points of resemblance between Spouse and friendly palpitating little gerbil, but fail. Spouse somehow irrevocably reptilian.

Time for mid-afternoon school run. Rise majestically from word processor. Wonder if the purchase of a gerbil would be an ecologically responsible act. Think perhaps not, unless free-range. Although the rodent exhibits useful paper and cardboard shredding functions. Wonder if Oliver North's life would have been easier with a gerbil, or possibly colony of gerbils, in his office.

Poised on doorstep when phone rings. It is Tom – who has not yet grasped the sacredness of the school-run hour. Typical non-parent.

'Listen,' he says menacingly, 'Nostradamus says the Third World War would start in the 1990s in the Middle East, as the result of some maniac. So can I come over tonight so we can go out in a blaze of glory?'

Issue evasive reply. Uneasily aware, all the way to school, that the innocent freedom of my gerbilline speculations has gone – probably for ever.

seventeen

OUTRAGED AT REPORTS OF abysmal ignorance of youth of today, inability of 5½% of population to name the Prime Minister, etc. Cannot imagine such an existence, though admit it has a certain louche charm, rather like the life of a cat.

Explain to Harriet that Daddy has gone to U.S.A. for a few months, show her it on the globe, and tell her that it is ruled over by a man called President Bush.

'Oh,' says Harriet with enthusiasm, 'is he Kate Bush's Daddy?' Henry asks if there is going to be a war and I reply firmly Not In Rusbridge and chivvy them off to bed.

'Mr de Santa Cruz! – Or may ah call you Count?' Mrs Pershing swept up the marble staircase to where Peveril was loitering majestically by a potted palm. 'May ah present mah daughter Donna?' panted the perspiration-bedewed matron. Donna Pershing's heavy eyelashes swept down like theatre curtains upon the powdered arena of her cheeks. Peveril gravely inclined his head.

But then, he was faced with the seemingly bottomless abyss of her cleavage. It reminded him of a ravine in the Smirnoff Mountains where, eighteen years ago, he had climbed with an intrepid friend from the Military Academy, Anatoly St Poges. They had camped in a cleft and dined off roasted goat and dewberries. A tear sprang to Peveril's eye at the memory of dear Anatoly, who had lost his life only two years later at the Uprising at Kremkraka.

Peveril closed his eyes and raised Donna Pershing's plump paw to his lips.

'We are so very honoured, Count, that a gentleman of your breedin' should deign to drop in at our modest li'l gatherin'.'

He loosened an acidic smile upon the Matron's lake of oily bonhomie, producing an effect fleetingly akin to salad dressing.

'We own a stud farm over at Great Heck. Ah do hope you'll see fit to drop by one day. Ah'd value your judgement on mah stallions.'

Peveril nodded. But the grotesque acreage of Mrs Pershing and her daughter no longer detained his eye.

It moved, mercurial and deft, over the ranks of bobbing and swirling girlhood on the dance floor below, but found nothing to detain it till, with a sudden flash, the face of Puce O'Dowd broke upon his alerted senses. She was idling by a pillar, fanning herself sulkily, and her eyes, when they found his, gleamed with the predatory phosphorescence of a swampsnake.

Doorbell interrupts Bonkbuster at this most promising moment. Irritation soon dissolves however at the sight of Tom, grinning from ear to ear, and bearing enormous bunch of chrysanths.

'Right,' he says, sweeping me into heavily pollinated embrace, 'let's get to grips with this Brave New World.'

Feel less than brave, however, at thought that children might awaken and descend to find Mummy in the arms of the plumber. Suggest tea first in case they are not quite asleep yet. Sod tea, says Tom, plenty of time for that when we're too old for sex. Reflect that perhaps my greater appetite for tea has sinister undertones.

Some quaint scruple prevents my admitting Tom to the matrimonial bedroom, sometimes known as the Master

Bedroom. We search in vain for the Mistress Bedroom. Agoraphobia soon renders the sofa uncomfortable for Tom's wild embraces. Finally lock ourselves in the bathroom and discover charming new use for lavatory: the Seat of Venus.

Reminded of Pope's or was it Dryden's line: 'Love hath set his palace in the place of excr – ' – or was it Yeats? Mind strangely inclined to wander. At Tom's profoundest groan, become convinced that I have introduced Puce O'Dowd too early.

Phone rings. Fly to answer it in case it is Spouse, which it is. Stupidly and unnecessarily (and, of course, guiltily) apologise for taking so long to answer it and explain seductively that I was in the loo having diarrhoea.

'Dai who?' quips Spouse merrily across the transatlantic ether. Privately lament that exposure to U.S.A. has already coarsened his wit.

eighteen

TOM OUTRAGED AT SUGGESTION that he should get out before dawn, as Mr Twill inclined to exercise his small whiskery terrier-thing along the pavement at first light. Have always prided myself on not giving a fig for what the neighbours think only to discover now that I care for little else. Children, in this respect, seem to be a particularly virulent form of neighbour.

'Look,' says Tom on the doorstep at 2 a.m., 'this isn't exactly what I had in mind. A quick grope in the bathroom and then kicked out in the middle of the night in case the kids wake up! Frankly, Dulcie, it's unworthy of you.'

Feel that perhaps what he really means is that it is unworthy of him. Assure him that more agreeable system will evolve.

'Don't cock it up,' he warns darkly. 'This is the right psychological moment to seize the nettle.'

Only able to nod dumbly, since all I am certain of is that four hours ago was the right psychological moment to hit the sack and close my eyes firmly for the night.

Awoken at 7 a.m. by Henry complaining that his inflatable Pink Panther has gone limp and can I do anything about it? Make feeble promise to restore aforementioned feline to turgidity.

Deposit children at school and return hoping for two hours' shuteye whilst Mrs Body Boldly Goes into fridge to sort out rapidly-developing environmental crisis there. Detained by sudden explosion of sentimentality on her part *vis-à-vis* Spouse. She doesn't half miss him and his little ways, I must be lorst poor thing without my better half and I bet the kiddies miss him somethink terrible eh poor little mites.

Tempted to dismiss all this hogwash with brisk Good Riddance line, but feel it is more diplomatic to smile sweetly and sigh, 'We'll struggle through,' à la Jill Archer. Have started listening to The Archers again in absence of Spouse. Am just thinking how much I hate them all except Nelson Gabriel when Mrs Body's words penetrate my mists of abstraction.

'Why don't you take a lodger dear? Use his study while he's away – look, get a little bed in there easy, give you peace of mind at nights and a few extra quid eh, why don't you?'

Graciously concede that proposal has a certain charm, and privately indulge in diverting series of speculations as to what sort of lodger most likely to give me peace of mind at nights.

Retreat for preprandial siesta – only sort available to parents of infant school children. Dream I discover whole wing of house previously undetected and am exploring it with exhilaration when phone wakes me. It is Saskia with news of unavoidable visit by her and Alice en route for Bath. Will have to nerve myself up for feminist verdict on my predicament.

Luxuriate awhile, wondering if dream about unsuspected wing of house symbolic of unawakened or unused parts of own psyche. Fear this could lead to course in Personal Growth. Privately wish to remain stunted. Pick nose in lovely silence. In absence of tissue, attach bogey to underside of bed. Clock strikes noon. Heigh-ho.

Have done absolutely nothing all day except recover from Gaudy Night. Not a word added to Bonkbuster. Peveril and Puce stalled at the very moment of that first magnetic flash of eye-contact. Probably the kindest thing one could do, in fact: after that moment it's downhill all the way.

Wonder if, in absence of Spouse, I am mysteriously turning into wrinkly teenager. Do not care. Adorable feeling, and very naughty in the caring sharing Nineties.

Get up finally in time to listen to Archers. No further prospect of sleep in any case, short of thinking about the E.R.M. or is it E.M.S.. Would soon tire of watching even Gordon Brown's lips talking about it.

Haul myself to the sink and immerse Pink Panther in cold water. Stream of bubbles emanates from his cranium, revealing fatal flaw in manufacture. Suspect I may be suffering from same.

Slope off at 2.45 to take Harriet to her first ballet lesson, and feel shudder of foreboding. Apparently most of her peers have been balleting away since birth. Convinced she will turn out to be leo(re)tarded.

nineteen

LOBBY OF SPORTS HALL swarming with venomous little girls all in leotards, tights and bandeaux of palest, most refined Kinnockian pink. Harriet's hair will not stay behind her bandeau but bounces out all over the place giving her air of demented gollywog.

Wonder if one is permitted to think the word *gollywog* these days let alone say it.

Harriet disappears behind curtains. Parents Requested Not

To Peep, even though we have shelled out best part of forty quid in fees and chic little pink tutus and doo-dahs. Mothers Wait Without, as usual throughout history.

Feel I would like a cup of coffee. Approach machine. Insert 20p as requested and Select Beverage. Empty cup drops down. Mutually puzzled pause. Find helpful button entitled Hot Water. Press it urgently. Scalding torrent descends – not, as hoped, into cup, but all over feet. Realise, too late, should have moved cup, after Selecting Beverage, to just below Hot Water Button.

Wonder if my degree of scientific comprehension is irrevocably pre-Aristotelian.

Am now proud owner of two scalded feet and one plastic cup containing one teaspoonful of brown powder. Manage to conceal swelling sense of achievement thereat, and throw it in the bin.

Limp bravely through lobby hoping other mothers have not noticed my débâcle with coffee machine, but sure they have. Little else to divert them here in this ante room to infant narcissism.

Recall, with foreboding, imminent visit of Alice and Saskia. Must hide Harriet's tutu. Trust Tom will not choose unfortunate moment to arrive with suitcases and amorous ultimatum.

Feel overpowering need for escapism. Sports Hall provides none save in form of publicity handouts scattered everywhere. Choose one advertising concert by rock group called Demented Carrot, and scribble furtively on reverse side.

'Ah declare, you must find our li'l country hop tedious after those Imperial Balls of yours at Saint Petersburg,' drawled Donna Pershing. They were leaning on a balustrade, looking down upon the dancing throng of Hicksville beaux and belles below. Peveril had never cherished exposure to mankind en masse and to him the vista of pulsating humanity below resembled nothing so much as a pan of Georgian goulash brought to a rolling boil.

Just such a stew Babuschka used to make for him on Friday nights, when his father and mother, ablaze with jewels, would go out to dine at Nitsky's and thence perchance to the theatre for the latest play by Dabitoff or Porky. Peveril's mother always wept at Dabitoff's The Sea Cow, but his father inclined more to the raw energy of Porky's Textiles, a modern play set in a corset factory.

Peveril sighed. He could not keep his mind on Donna Pershing even for twenty seconds, and he was sure that, if the opportunity arose, he would be able to keep his body on her for even less. Why, he would rather think of Babuschka, silently embroidering her cambric funeral pillows, her dear old face creased into perplexity like a map of Transdanubia after partition.

But one glance here in Hicksville had disturbed him. For a split second he had been rocketed back into the here-and-now.

'Tell me, Miss Pershing,' he said in a casual way, blowing a stream of cigar smoke out across the rising miasma of sweat and scent, 'who's that girl with the ill-tempered face? The one lurking by that pillar down there? She seems – well, apart from it all, somehow.'

'Oh, Lawd, Count, you'd better steer clear of her. She's nothin' but trouble. Three beaux from Filbert County throwd themselves into the Rushdie River on account o'her. That's Puce O'Dowd!'

Peveril stared down at Puce O'Dowd with reinforced interest. Such a very short, bald, common name! He felt his surplus syllables tighten chivalrously at the sight of her strange haunted fa –

'Mummy! Where's my Mars bar?'

Harriet leaps onto my knee with the thistledown grace of a Challenger Tank. End of idyll.

twenty

SPOUSE RINGS TO COMPLAIN he is sick of smoked salmon and scrambled eggs for breakfast and TV evangelists urging him to donate his body, soul and bank balance to the Almighty. Express sympathy. Admit that no-one has asked me for my soul recently and that I don't have a bank balance any more. Remain tactfully silent on subject of body. Spouse promises to send a few dollars as soon as he gets his hands on any, asks me to kiss the children for him, and rings off.

Reflect that kiss a difficult transaction when participants separated by over two thousand miles but nevertheless probably Spouse's favourite form of salutation. He does not, however, request me to kiss myself for him. Ay me.

Console myself with charity Christmas catalogues. Order, for Great Aunt Elspeth, tea-caddy hand-carved in India – one hopes, by someone over sixteen. For Spouse, select amazing digital clock powered by bananas: for Tom, Red Ragweave Rucksack, partly in case he ever feels the urge to Move On, and partly for the sheer alliteration of it. For Henry, 'Carry on Disarming' Video, though fear it will fall on deaf ears, and for Harriet, racoon fluppet with sinister warning, 'it comes to life in your hands.'

Why fluppet? Why not puppet? Is fluppet a puppet with a fatal flaw? E.g. No orifice? If so, envy it. How simple such a life would be.

Realise have not ordered anything for self, so plump for bulk purchase of personalised recycled bogrolls complete with logo: *Save Trees – Wipe Your Bum on a Dockleaf.*

Hallucinating by now, I turn to latest and most hardcore Green catalogue which urges me to turn my old newspapers into bricks that will burn as long as a lump of coal. Mind boggles, but not sure how useful this exercise would be as the only place I could burn anything at all is the garden – apart from chichi little incense burner on my desk in shape of Buddha and faintly resembling Norman Willis: present from Tom and never used.

Mind, already boggling, actually bursts at the thought of *Re-usable Sanitary Pads.* But then, why not? Terribly Georgian, and surely preferable to the 750 million disposable ones clogging up every sewage outlet in the land, choking fish and mystifying children. Order some, though hope that onset and completion of menopause is feasible by Friday.

Exhausted by catalogues, stagger from study in search of plastic, lipstick, or gin and tonic. Settle for cup of decaffeinated Earl Grey. Must, after picking up kids from school, perform shopping raid on Green Light Health Food Shop as Alice and Saskia arrive tonight and, despite their distaste for female domestic servitude, will expect soya bean and nettle casserole to be steaming on the table.

Time for brief mental excursion to Marlon County. Must rescue Peveril from company of tedious blubbery Southern Belle Donna Pershing.

Peveril hacked through the chestnut grove, admiring the supple grace of the sable hunter between his thighs. Old Mrs Pershing certainly knew her horseflesh. And they had killed a hog in his honour, and the resulting Gammon and Beans had been acceptable, though more appropriate on a peasant's table in his native land. He thrust from his memory the scent of a table at Nitsky's in St Petersburg, with the Crème Brûlée glittering like brown enamel beneath the flickering chandeliers.

And then, all of a sudden, the glimmer of water showed among some trees to his right. Peveril knew his mount was thirsty, so they left the gallop and made for the lake. But what was this? The sound of girlish laughter rang out across the water, and Peveril's horse pulled up beside a tumbled heap of muslin: maidenly clothes, evidently discarded in the sticky heat. Peveril silently slipped from the saddle and got out his –

Phone rings. It is Tom requesting glimpse of me tonight. Regret it will be impossible due to presence of Alice and Saskia.

'Don't you want me to meet your friends, then?' he asks, with strangely plangent dying fall suggestive of animal with no backbone. Floppet, perhaps. Confident however that he will still Come to Life in My Hands.

'Yes, but later.' Briskly change subject to own financial instability, and amusing suggestion by Mrs Body that I should take a lodger.

'What a brilliant idea!' cries Tom. 'Take me!'

twenty-one

*Peveril got out his flask of Kaiser Helmut Apricot Brandy,
leaned against a savannah oak and breathed deeply. The scent of the
swamp-rose filled his nostrils, and playful splashing mingled with the
drowsy afternoon drone of the cottonseed bugs and the occasional deep
croak of Boothby's Thunder Toad in his hole up the creek.*

*Peveril sighed. There was something heavy and velvety about this
southern air that seemed to drag him down, down towards – he knew
not what. He flung himself prone upon a lush carpet of vegetation and
for a moment closed his eyes and surrendered to lethargy. But all too
soon he was jerked from his reverie by an abrupt and challenging cry.*

*'If you was a real gen'leman, yo'd ride off right now with yo' eyes
closed, 'stead o'lurkin' in that poison ivy like a goddam rattlesnake.'*

*There, standing waist deep and naked in the lake, her modesty
preserved by the dark streams of hair that clung to her womanly form,
her extraordinary face alight with indignation, stood – Puce
O'Dowd.*

Reluctantly forced to abandon Bonkbuster by imminent
arrival of Alice and Saskia on 2.35 p.m. train. Hide Bonkbuster. Hide *Vogues*. Hide barbaric and sinful Barbies and Sindies.
Stick head round Henry's bedroom door but conclude that
arms proliferation within has gone beyond possibility of
concealment and pin large KEEP OUT notice on door, complete
with radioactive symbol.

Prepare Vegan stew which resembles stagnant village pond
in need of reclamation. Feel it would be vastly improved by
addition of few old bones as in bona fide village ponds, but
refrain. No old bones in house anyway except those secreted
so well beneath piles of cellulite in yours truly.

On way to station, buy *Wright's Vaporiser*, recommended
by Mrs Body upon hearing Harriet's cough – a sound resembling the collapse of the walls of Jericho. Had heard of
Wright's Vaporiser but had somehow assumed it was part of

the Industrial Revolution – perhaps precursor to Puffing Billy or Spinning Jenny.

Collect Alice and Saskia from station and then Henry and Harriet from school. Saskia makes fatal enquiry characteristic of the non-parent: What Did You Do At School Today Henry? Henry picks his nose and says I Forget Can We Have Monster Munches Mum? This concludes attempt of my companions to talk amongst themselves. Thereafter they all address me simultaneously and individually rather like baroque quartet from, say, the Barrage of Virago. (Henry here the token man, but sung in performance by butch mezzo.)

Detect in myself a waning of appetite for adult conversation. Often notice this when visitors come. On other hand, have little desire for childish conversation either. Suspect the old bones are turning into stalks – i.e. am becoming a vegetable.

On arrival at Cranford Gardens, Saskia presents Harriet with carved polyp – allegedly a rabbit – product of Third World job creation scheme. 'Don't worry,' Saskia adds hurriedly, 'it's teak from a Managed Plantation.' What was really worrying me was whether Harriet could make a brave stab at facial expression suggestive of pleasure. Alas, her face falls several fathoms and she cries Where Have You Put My Sindies Mummy?! – in direct contravention of U.N. Resolution 2637498 promising not to mention Sindies in presence of Alice and Saskia.

Luckily Alice and Saskia did not hear as they were performing Mozartian duet about quite wonderful gamelan Ensemble from somewhere down in Devon which I must go and hear because it will ravish my eardrums.

Nod in parody of assent. Secretly convinced that my eardrums are suffering from overkill already and what they really crave is two sides of wall-to-wall Walkman silence.

Phone rings and I fly to it, hoping it is a Heavy Breather but alas, it is the opposite – i.e. Spouse eager to unload latest ungrateful sneers about American culture. Alice and Saskia ignore his telephonic intervention and continue to talk at me throughout call – for all the world as though he were actually present.

After his call, spend a divine five minutes of silence alone in the lavatory.

twenty-two

ALICE OFFERS 'TO DO the washing-up' – i.e. sit chortling patronisingly over *The Rusbridge Gazette* and scattering fag-ash everywhere – whilst I put Harriet to bed. Henry has already 'gone to bed' – i.e. is performing series of arms sales behind closed doors to unstable puppet and teddy bear regimes. Saskia declares she will come and 'help' me put Harriet to bed. Harriet promises she 'will be good for ever and ever' if she can have a My Little Phoney Equestrian Experience. Pronounce veto, whereat she collapses into aria of heartrending coughing.

We go upstairs. On the third stair my mind inexplicably retreats from Saskia's ongoing lecture on Population Control and Harriet's equine whine, and tip-toes back towards Bonkbuster, stalled at moment when Puce O'Dowd rises like The Lady of the Lake before Peveril's enchanted gaze.

'Madam,' murmured Peveril, averting his gaze chivalrously towards a riotous tangle of swamp jasmine, 'allow me to –'

'Mummeeee! Gabrielle has got *three* My Little Ponies! 'Snot fair!'

'And did you know,' Saskia persists, 'that it takes less than five days for the world population to increase by a million?'

Am somehow surprised to find we have only got as far as the bathroom. Immerse Harriet in clouds of cheap bubble-bath (hastily decanted into Body Shop bottles before Saskia's arrival). Harriet frolics in the foam like Blake mezzotint of a sprite. Admire her – not too obviously I hope.

'It's an extra 85 million people a year, Dulcie, did you know that?'

Did not. Would rather know what mezzotint was, frankly. Sigh and feel guilty. Tempted to point out that my personal exertions have only increased world population by two, but refrain. Alice and Saskia after all produce nothing more environmentally harmful than diatribes.

'Mummeeee! Emily's got a My Little Pony and when you wind it up its tail whizzes round!'

Attempt to set up Wright's Vaporiser. Instructions terrify. 'Take care to prevent spillage. Should spillage occur, remove contaminated clothing and wash the skin at once.' Have spent my entire life taking care to prevent spillage, but in vain. Decide to Do It Over The Wash-basin.

'Mexico City's going to have 26 million by the year 2000 and already two million – two million, Dulcie! – haven't even got a water supply.' Feel guilty about wash-basin, even though cracked.

'Allow me to withdraw. Not for a moment would I dream of inconveniencing a lady at her toilet.'

'Toilet nothin'!' drawled Puce O'Dowd with a satiric grin. 'We was jus' skinny-dippin'.'

Peveril shuddered at her coarse idiom, and yet –

'Now I must wash your hair, darling.'

'No! No! No! I hate it!'

Approach Harriet with bottle, but realise in the nick of time it is Wright's Vaporiser Fluid which must at all times be Kept Away From Children. Shudder, and replace it with Grapefruit Shampoo. Feel sure grapefruit would be better employed nourishing Egypt's extra-million-people-every-two-months.

Harriet successfully shampooed, dried, nightied and immobilised in cloud of vapour, though Saskia talks all the way through *Towser and the Terrible Thing*. Stick head round Henry's bedroom door and inform him in deep growl that if he is not in bed in two minutes there will be No Telly next Saturday.

Exhausted by my failure to cope with my two, wonder how Nigeria manages with her 100 million. Express hope that Alice has made a cup of coffee.

'Oh no,' says Saskia. 'The coffee trade is the most gigantic exploitation of Third World Labour.'

Fear it will be Barley Cup, untouched since their last visit. Hope it has not gone off, though not sure how one could ever tell.

Peveril leapt onto His Little Pony and galloped away into the languorous vapour of the Georgia afternoon.

twenty-three

PEVERIL SAT ALONE ON *the verandah of the old clapboard Dower House which Cyrus J. Pershing had placed at his disposal. Half a mile away the Pershing mansion glimmered in the moonlight among the sweet chestnut trees. It was near midnight: the Pershings must all be abed. But Peveril was restless. He tossed the butt of his Havana cigar away into the handsome old Barbara bush rose. It glowed for a moment, then surrendered to the dark.*

'How . . . how something or other,' thought Peveril. He was aware of a deep uneasiness at the heart of things. 'Dmitri!' he called, and at the other end of the verandah, something stirred.

The boy had been asleep. Peveril was touched by the childlike heaviness of his face.

'Dmitri,' said Peveril, 'Fetch me a glass of the Delors Cognac. I am sick at heart. I know not why.'

'If you ask me,' commented Dmitri in his rough Georgian way, 'what you need is a good Szbltchchnik – nokplonky!

For a moment, fear Dmitri may have lapsed into the argot of

his native Tbspsvili, then realise word processor has gone on the blink. Message appears on screen: *printer failed*. A bit terse, I feel. No hint of apology, no music to soothe jangled nerves, no Michael Buerk with a quizzical, 'I'm sorry, we seem to have lost that report.'

Phone five computer firms but my request that they should send a man round immediately is greeted with derision and besides, they point out I am not IBM compatible. It seems I have no alternative but to take the wretched thing back to where I bought it – i.e. Swindon, a round trip of more than two hours. Necessity of collecting children from school in one and a half hours an impediment to these plans.

Who could collect kids? Mrs Body is on her annual trip to Playa de Las Americas. Do not relish the thought of Mr Twill chauffeuring my darlings as he might have another heart attack at the wheel. Mrs Twill only drove once, in 1957, and it brought her out in prickly heat. Typical of Alice and Saskia to depart three hours precisely before their presence could have become constructive.

Phone rings. Answer with crocodilian snap that this is Domum, as if I am some public school prefect.

'Hey! You sound as if you need some cuddling therapy. Shall I come round? I'm between jobs.'

Vent anti-word processor spleen and Tom cheerfully offers to collect kids, take 'em home, feed 'em, etc., etc. He has a key already, remember, no sweat.

Expel from my mind all thoughts of perspiration and drive to Swindon on wave of gratitude. Had been keeping Tom at arm's length recently because of visit of Alice and Saskia and also out of pusillanimous bourgeois guilt. What do I care what the neighbours say? What a gem he is, etc., etc.

Wagnerian sunlight plays upon late autumn landscape: ploughed fields suggest new start, etc. Turn corner with unusual sweeping abandon and hear word processor fall on its face in back of car. Do not stop. After all, I'm taking it to be mended anyway. It can just be mended, if necessary, even more.

On way home, buy bottle of Muscadet. Arrive to find real fire lit in sitting room for first time for four years. Children and Tom making robot out of old cornflake packet and bogrolls. Whole firelit scene resembles seventeenth century Flemish genre painting – apart from Henry's Mutant Turtle sweatshirt.

'Tom's going to put us to bed!' bawls Harriet in ecstasy.

'They've had a big tea,' says Tom, 'and there's Lasagne in the oven for us, later.' My nostrils confirm this happy state of affairs. 'Let me get you a cuppa,' continues this paragon, and then stops by the door. 'I've taken the liberty of installing my sleeping bag in your husband's study. Just in case you need any help in the night.'

Give in gracefully and relax by fire. Feel that my last qualms must perforce melt before this relentlessly delightful diet of tea, lasagne, childcare and *Szbltchchnik – nokplonky!*

twenty-four

'HAVING TROUBLE WITH YOUR pipes again, Mrs Domum?' enquires Mr Twill with sudden mischievous panache as we collide upon the pavement. Bestow polite smile on him, though scent danger. 'Thought I saw that plumber johnnie of yours round here again yesterday.'

'Oh! Tom. Yes.' Assume casual and dismissive air, though suspect it is at odds with high tide blush which rushes all over face, hair, pavement, and possibly East Anglia. 'It was my cleaner's idea. Mrs Body. She said Why don't you get a lodger whilst your husband's away. Tom needed somewhere for a few weeks whilst he and his girlfriend get their new flat ready.'

'Ah – the girlfriend's staying with you, too?'

'No – ' Another blush races across face of earth, inundating the Seychelles. 'No – she's staying with her mother. She's . . . not been well.'

'The gel's not well? Oh dear.'

'No. The girl's all right. Her mother's been a bit ill. She – well she had a hysterectomy. She'll soon be on her feet again.'

'So meanwhile the daughter's helping her mother out? Must be a decent gel. Don't hear of many young people like that nowadays. Good show. Ah, well. Must be going.'

He tips his tweed pork pie hat to me and resumes his walk, his small whiskery crypto–dog Hamish straining at the leash. Leap into car and endure moment of intense intellectual exhaustion. Clear debris, including Mr Potato Head, from back seat to make room for children.

Peveril looked into Dmitri's taunting green eyes. He sometimes wondered –

Sod off, Peveril. I've got enough fiction on my hands right now without having to follow your tedious pre-coital ramblings.

All the way to school, however, retain mysterious urge to return to Peveril's verandah, to sip cognac with him, discuss the inconveniences of Eros, and to admire the tumbled peasant comeliness of the drowsing Dmitri.

'Mummeee! Mr Potato Head's lost his eyes!'

'Ah, no, darling – don't worry. He hasn't actually *lost* them, just . . . just lent them to a passing parsnip.'

'What parsnip?'

'Er, well a poor old parsnip, you know, struggling along, and he said to Mr Potato Head, *I'm trying to find my way to the soup, but I can't see a thing.* So Mr P –'

'Waaaaa! Poor parsnip! Won't *ever* eat soup again!'

So. My most agile fictional reassurances end not in infantile satisfaction but in new visions of horror. Harriet cries all the way home.

Henry says Can we have Alphabites beans and sausages for tea Mum? Reply yes, uneasily aware that only alternative is parsnip soup and there are no sausages within fifty yards of the house.

Stop at Spar to buy sausages. Decide to save soup for Tom

and me to have later when children are in bed. Wonder if they get Greek Alphabites at Eton and Harrod's. I mean, Harrow.

Understandably fatigued. Tom puts children to bed again, earning more Brownie points – though he does not approve of Brownies and prefers pacifist organisation called something like Woodland Folk. I doze by the fire, though alas without revealing my peasant comeliness.

On Tom's return downstairs, inform him that I have invented for him a girlfriend, the girlfriend's mother, and the girlfriend's mother's hysterectomy. Tom looks severe and says, Look here Dulcie, I've heard about this course I think you should go on, it's all about Personal Growth and Development.

Phone rings. It is Spouse. Tom goes off tactfully to warm up soup. Spouse grumbles about inability of Winnesota freshmen to do joined-up writing. Nerving myself up for extraordinary effort, tell him I'm thinking of getting a tenant, preferably a man, to keep an eye on things whilst he's away.

Spouse ignores this announcement and asks if I can have a look round his study for photocopies of two seventeenth century texts, *A Second Fiery Flying Roll* by Abiezer Coppe, and *The Bloudy Vision of John Farley* by Arise Evans, and fax them to him at Winnesota. Observe that Flying Roll sounds like seventeenth century equivalent of fax, whereat Spouse laughs and says O for a woman with wit.

Wonder if this was a compliment, or quite the contrary.

twenty-five

ONLY THREE WEEKS TILL Christmas!' cries Henry with sadistic glee, leaping on my head at dawn. Harriet asks if she may have a Three Wishes Sindy. Assert that I myself also have three wishes: a)that they will shut up b)that they will go away c)that I may enjoy another ten minutes' peace before getting up. O.K. Mum they cry We'll go and torment Tom instead.

Tom, in sleeping bag on floor of Spouse's study, has endured this treatment for the past fortnight without complaint. Wonder if this man has any flaws. Then recall that I am well aware of several.

For example, last night over cocoa he produces old copy of magazine called *Resurgence*. Odd title. Sounds like unfortunate gastric condition. Magazine full of green articles by people like Parkin, Porritt, Odent. Lovely illustrations, nice thick paper. Even poem on *Zen and the Art of Apple Pie Making*.

'But this is what you really need, Dulcie,' Tom points urgently to advertisement for Residential weekend course called Inner Journey to the Higher Self, promising to work on Sensitivity and the Intuitive Faculty. My own intuitive faculty warns me that I have no Higher Self, but do not dare to say so.

'This is the one I really fancy,' Tom goes on. '*The Karmic Journey*: exploring Karma and past lives through meditation and conscious regression with Judy Hall.'

Had to admit that one sounded tempting, though felt a pang of jealousy at the thought of Tom experiencing conscious regression with a Judy Hall. Past lives! Yes please. Would like nothing more than to explore a past life, preferably one without children, housework, cooking, G.B.H., H.I.V., G.C.S.E., E.M.S., E.R.M., E.M.U., N.S.U., N.F.U. and above all E.C.U.

Perhaps this is why I am a writer of romantico–historico fiction. The exploration of alternative past lives. Admire this thought for a moment as shaft of brilliant insight but soon realise it is banal cliché like all my other such shafts.

Idly flip through copy of *Resurgence*, still by bed, and am beguiled at thought of Magical Voice Techniques, Tibetan and Mongolian overtone chanting. Might try it instead of my habitual chant: *Get dressed now I won't tell you again did you hear what I said Henry get dressed Now! I shall get cross in a minute Get*

Dressed Now! We'll be late if you don't and you know how you hate being late Do You Want A SMACK? GET DRESSED NOW!!

Diverted at another theory proposed: that Your Style of Thinking Colours Your Mind. Fear, alas, that mine is colour described in the Next Catalogue as Taupe, i.e. the colour of Nau Haupe.

Whatever am I going to do about this ongoing Tom-Sleeping-On-Spouse's-Study-Floor Situation?

Allow myself to be distracted by advert for Shiatsu course. Ad features drawing of person apparently strangling someone lying on the floor. Fear that neither Shiatsu nor strangling will supply the answer to my dilemma.

Toss *Resurgence* aside, though reverently – not with the contemptuous impatience with which I toss aside, say, *Harper's*. Stare at ceiling, and discern upon it a crack shaped like the Mississippi River.

Peveril stirred on his verandah. (Am I ever going to get him off that damned verandah?) *He must have slept. His grandfather's Fabergé fob watch informed him it was 3 a.m. Far away in the velvety Georgia night, a paddlesteamer hooted on its way down the Rushdie River to the Mississippi.* (Mem: research: did paddlesteamers hoot? Does Mississippi flow through, or near Georgia? Inconvenience of past lives: saturation in detail of which one is unfortunately entirely ignorant.)

Am drifting away down Mississippi on raft steered mysteriously but satisfactorily by Imran Khan, possibly on journey towards Inner Self, when Tom sticks his head round bedroom door and says,

'You have a lie-in, darling. I'll get them off to school.'

Think perhaps I can ignore Tom's eccentricities, and drift gratefully back to sleep. But alas. Imran has been replaced by John Major and raft appears to be sinking. Awake with headache at 9.30. Annoyed. Very remiss of subconscious to serve up dream about economics when all that was required was sex or cricket.

twenty-six

TOM'S FRIEND DOG EXPECTED for one night en route to Glastonbury. Tom says he'll see to it all: Dog can sleep on floor of Futility Room, no problem, and he, Tom, will organise supper, get another Fasta Pasta Dish from *Green Light Food To Go*. I am absolutely to go to bed the minute I feel tired and besides, Dog can do my horoscope as he is an ace star gazer.

Henry and Harriet not enchanted by Dog ('HE SMELLS Mummy') ('Sssh! It's only patchouli'). Dog not child-oriented, and is too busy working out my astral conjunctions to be interested in Ninja Turtles. Have to inform him of exact minute, let alone year, of birth, and trust he will not tell Tom.

Once children in bed and Fasta Pasta despatched, my planets are scrutinised. Dog informs me that Saturn has now passed out of my fifth house and things should be much easier. Tom looks complacent: clearly thinks this a reference to the departure of Spouse. Stay up much too late poring over my cusps. Alarmed by Dog's assurance that I have great spiritual resonance. Retire at midnight leaving the young men to roll their own and philosophise till dawn.

'Mummeeeee!'

Summoned by bawls at 2.15 a.m. Stagger to Harriet's bedside and enquire brusquely whether pee, drink or dream-exorcism is required.

'Ear! Ear hurts! Come in *your* bed!'

Give in instantly as freezing, and install her beside me, where she moans and thrashes for three hours. Give her two tsps. of Calpol and take six myself. Place Mummy's magic hand over the offending orifice but my spiritual resonance seems to be wearing thin.

'Ear hurts! Ear hurts! Wish I'd never been *born*!'

Can only persuade her that survival is desirable by heroic-ally spinning series of inspiring yarns in which turtles, bats, elephants, etc., have their earache cured by helpful singing worms, the West Wind, women in grey suits, etc. What you might call the aural tradition.

Reflect bitterly that if Saturn had not moved out of my fifth house he could at least have taken over at 4.30 a.m.

'Oh dear,' says Harriet suddenly at 4.45, leans out of bed and is sick all over bedside phone, my slippers, and Simon Schama's *Citizens* – Spouse's parting gift to me, and still alas unread. Whilst I am mopping up, Harriet enquires how you spell *cauliflower*. Assume this is sign of recovery and indeed she falls asleep before I reach the W.

Awoken twenty minutes later by Henry who complains that he had a horrid dream in which I was possessed by the Devil, my face turned green, black custard came out of my mouth and my face fell off. Observe that this may well be my destiny if I get no sleep at all tonight. Harry demands access to my bed too or Snot Fair.

Leave Henry and Harriet snoring in unison in matrimonial bed, creep to children's room and slump gratefully into lower bunk. Have just reached arms of Morpheus (6.30ish I should think) when phone rings. Reach out to grab it with eyes closed, thinking I am in own bed, and dislocate knuckles on wall. Realise dimly where I am, leap to escape and strike head on upper bunk.

Sit still on edge of bunk and see stars. Vaguely aware phone has stopped ringing. See stripes.

Peveril was awoken by the harsh cry of the Marsh Gibbon. For an instant a damp cramp seized his limbs, and he knew not where he was. At the summerhouse by Lake Virol? On manoeuvres in the Blishen Forest? Camping with –

'Good mawnin', Mistah de Santa Cruz,' came a light, taunting voice. And Peveril recollected, with a shudder, that he was in the wrong Georgia.

Arrive in own bedroom to find Harriet replacing phone. She looks stern.

'That was Daddy,' she said. 'I told him you'd gone away and left us. And the phone's covered with sick.'

Commiserate whilst putting on my slippers only to discover that they are, too.

'How extraordinary,' says Tom later. 'I slept through the whole thing.' Good job he's a bloody paragon.

twenty-seven

PLAGUED BY VAGUE FEELING of loss. Read somewhere that somewhere-or-other (evidence of aluminium saucepans, here, alas) anyway in a foreign country somewhere they've banned TV advertising of toys in the run-up to Christmas. Experience intense desire to emigrate thither. Henry and Harriet, glued to box on Saturday morning, set up antiphonal chant of greed:

'I want Precious Places! I want Three Wishes Sindy!'

'I want a Spirograph! I want –'

Feel moved to declare personal War on I Want.

However, secretly appalled and guilty that I have not yet so much as bought a bag of nuts.

Anxiety increases upon revelation that Father Christmas is to adorn Rusbridge Christmas Bonanza and will be At Home in the Reference Library from 4.30 – 6.00 p.m. No doubt he will feel at ease there amongst all the other bearded down-and-outs.

Bribe Henry not to give the game away, but fear this will be the last Christmas during which Harriet believes in Santa. Plagued anew by vague sense of loss. But on the other hand, why should the bearded git get all the credit when I'm the one who sits up till 2 a.m. putting those last, loving artistic little touches to the begging letter to the Bank Manager?

Have only £6.20 in purse. Doubt if it is enough to get us through Rusbridge Christmas Bonanza night out and wonder if Santa will accept Visa. Strange to recollect, I was paid just over £6 a week for a mornings-only vacation job doing clerical work, twenty years ago. But that was when we still had our halfcrowns and shillings and farthings and furlongs and rods and pecks and bushels and Beatles. Experience vague, persistent, but still unfocused sense of loss.

Centre of Rusbridge seems to have been gift-wrapped by someone with questionable taste. Number of Olde-Worlde stalls erected in Market Place with people in Victorian dress selling stuffed toys, most of which resemble Geoffrey Howe.

Harriet demands access to Bran Tub, except it is Expanded Polystyrene Tub these days.

'Oh Christ!' she exclaims on unwrapping gift. 'It's only a pencil sharpener.'

'Don't say *Christ*, darling.'

Proceed to Santa's Grotto or perhaps Clauset, and queue for 2½ hours behind plump young wench with crewcut accompanied by two very naughty little boys. Convinced it is Clarrie Grundy for few seconds before recalling that Clarrie Grundy is fictional. Experience renewed sense of loss and fear it may be related to marbles.

Santa – jolly man who usually presides over Health Food Shop – sternly enjoins Harriet to Be Good Till Christmas and gives her a promisingly large parcel. She opens it outside under street lamp, to reveal a toy dustpan and brush.

'Oh Christ!'

'Don't say *Christ*, Mummy!'

Henry, who submitted to audience with the Great Man for the sake of material gain, emerges with enormous tube of sweets containing sugar, glucose syrup, hydrogenated vegetable oil, citric acid, modified starch, flavourings, gelatine, acidity regulator: sodium citrate, colours: ponceau 4R, quinoline yellow, beta-carotene, indigo carmine, and glazing agent: carnauba wax. Wonder if Santa will ever be able to hold his head up in the Health Food Shop again. Also wonder if I can contrive to introduce into the Bonkbuster a character named Ponceau Carnauba.

Henry says Snot Fair she's got a toy and I've only got sweets. Harriet says Snot Fair I want sweets too. Distract her by suggesting she should christen her new dustpan and brush by sweeping up the debris in the Market Square but unfortunately in the early stages of the operation she has a close encounter of the turd kind. O Christ again.

Realise that the only references made to the Messiah during the whole event were at moments of disappointment or outrage. Wonder if vague but persistent sense of loss could be related to total absence of Christ from Christmas. Distressed when penny finally drops: 'tis not the Messiah that I miss, but Margaret Thatcher.

twenty-eight

SEVERAL TRANSATLANTIC PHONE CALLS have established that we cannot possibly afford to meet Spouse in Disney World for what one imagines would have been surpassingly vulgar series of Yuletide Experiences. Spouse therefore has no alternative but to come over here for a few days.

'Quite frankly,' he sighs 'by the time I've got over my jet lag, it'll be time to go back again.'

Cannot imagine jet lag would offer very different prospect from Spouse's usual demeanour.

Urgent necessity therefore of evicting Tom from floor of Spouse's study, albeit temporarily.

Tom uncooperative. He had been looking forward to Christmas with the kids: he had (or had I forgot?) bought and decorated Christmas tree, acquired Christmas pudding containing no animal fats from Green Light Food To Go, etc., etc. And was he now to be slung out on his ear on a cold, dark, December night just because a mere Spouse looms?

Answer: profuse apologies but Yes.

Tom points out that Spouse will be so tired he'll probably not even notice there's something unusual on his study floor. Shake my head. Tom gets on high horse and makes moral speech about Honesty and Clarity and Seizing the Opportunity and Face to Face Adult Conversations and Reaching New Understanding and Ushering in New Era. Am reminded briefly of Queen's Christmas message but insist We Don't Want to Lose You But We Think You Ought to Go.

'All right then I bloody well will – right now!' cries Tom, flings out of house and slams front door. This inconvenient as tomorrow I have to make last-minute trip to London for publisher's party and had hoped that Tom would be there to immobilise and defuse children. Make instead complex arrangements with Mrs Body, who warns me that her Stan has given her the hump something cruel. Assure her that this is what husbands are for.

Leap aboard London train with customary feeling of escape and sink instantly into Bonkbuster.

'So! You're the Russian Count the whole of Marlon County's talkin' about.' Peveril looked into the taunting green eyes of Puce O'Dowd. 'Ah declare, ah never dreamed a gentleman like you would sleep outdoors.'

'My dear child,' drawled Peveril, trying to conceal a spasm of cramp in his hams, the inevitable result of a night on the verandah, 'I have slept under the bitter stars on the plains of Amstrad; in a wolf-hide bivouac in the Albanberg mountains, and, in the duck-shooting season, in a freezing punt on Lake Virol. To doze through one of your warm Georgia nights is naught but a pleasure to your humble servant. Forgive me for not rising.'

'I'm just a-walkin' over to see Donna,' Puce O'Dowd's features slipped into a cunning grin. 'Folks do say as you-all'll be engaged to her 'fore the Fall.'

'I beg your pardon, Madam?' Peveril was not entirely at ease with her earthy diction. Puce winked.

'Jus' call me Puce . . . Puce O'Dowd. I don' b'lieve as we've been introduced.'

She extended a swarthy paw.

Peveril leapt to his feet, his kneecaps giving out a deafening report that echoed among the groves of sweet chestnuts and brought Dmitri running out onto the verandah. Peveril took her hand: it smelt of tobacco and sweet violets. Slowly, with a fiery inevitability like the burning sun going down on the snakelike blue coils of the Rushdie River, Peveril's lips sank onto the most accessible of her veins.

'Just call me Count,' said Peveril. 'And I hope you will join me for breakfast. Dmitri! Bring coffee!'

'Fergive me!' her breath swirled up into his face like the exhalation of an orchid, 'but ah mustn't be late for Donna. An' fergive me, Count if I 'dvise you not to sleep on th'verandah tonight. Ah've got a wild, wild cousin who'll be strayin' thisaways, 'bout midnight. His name is Ponceau Carnauba.' And with a strange alluring toss of the head, she was gone.

On the way back, spend some time in bookstall on Swindon Station. Very struck by magazine cover photo of John Malkovich apparently picking his nose. Wish he would pick mine.

twenty-nine

INFORM SPOUSE I AM suffering from post-Noel depression. He replies Mmmmn-hmmmn? (strange, and irritating transatlantic grunt he has picked up: a kind of reluctant hello-but-I'll-keep-you-at-arm's-length-for-a-few-more-seconds-while-I-finish-this-editorial-and-pick-my-nose sort of noise.)

'Never mind,' I sigh. 'Nobody ever listens to me.'

'Post-Christmas Blues? Yule get over it,' he affirms, and promptly falls asleep for the third time today.

Spouse behaving as though jet lag were his own unique tragedy rather than a universal inconvenience. Sigh again, rather more martyredly, and survey widespread chaos, in midst of which Harriet sits watching video of Spiderwoman destroying vast life-threatening mummy.

'Harriet! Will you please clear away this LEGO stuff? Or I'll trip on it and bash my brains out!'

'Puddun?'

Since her ear infection Harriet has developed Beethovian tendencies. Fear she may, after all, need grommets, despite my blithe scorn on the subject when the Health Visitor called some aeons ago. Serve me right. (Such a comforting reflection for a liberal.)

'Switch off the telly and clear up this mess!'

'Puddun?'

Am reminded of favourite line by Jilly Cooper: 'Mummy says pardon is a much worse word than fuck.' Glad I do not care if Harriet says pardon. As long as she grows out of it eventually.

Henry comes in wearing new Transatlantic Walkman. His arrival co-incides with particularly ear-splitting disintegration of one of Spiderwoman's mummies.

'Mum! I've lost my marbles!'

'Hah!' I explete. '*You* think *you've* lost *your* marbles!'

'What?'

'Take those blasted headphones off when I'm talking to you!'

Alarmed at news however as lost marbles even more likely to lead to broken femur which, in Spouse's case, could prevent his return to U.S.A. and issue in era of endless nursing.

No word from Tom for ages and am slightly alarmed to find I am only slightly alarmed.

Suddenly lose rag and switch TV off in midst of Spider-woman's transformation from tough, aggressive inter-galactic warrior to teetering high-heeled ninny, her Alter Ego – without which she could never get by in regular society.

'Aaaaaauw! Snot Fair! I hate you!'

Harriet darts me look of revulsion normally reserved for vast life-threatening mummies.

'Clear up this mess, NOW!' Change tack rapidly as cannot

face yet more tears and tantrums. 'And if you do, you can have a treat.'

'What? A Sindy Princess?'

'NO not a sodding Sindy! An ear test!'

'Puddun?'

Novel idea of ear test appeals, however, and LEGO civilisation is swept away into a shoebox – too good a destiny for our own, I fear.

Install Harriet at far end of room with her back to me, then cannot think of anything to whisper.

'Mummy! Have you gone?'

'No, wait. . . .'

Spy last chocolate bar lying on floor covered with pine needles. Aware that offering her something delicious would be best form of ear test.

'Harriet . . . would you like a Wispa?'

Henry pounces on me, Yes Please Mum!

'Shut up you! And put your blasted Walkman back on! Now, Shh!'

Peace prevails for a split second. Spouse wakes up with a start.

'What the hell was that?'

'Puddun?'

'That,' I explain, 'was silence.'

When children are in bed, Spouse begs me to go and get us a bottle of Bushmills.

In darkness of hall, trip on marbles, bash brains out against radiator and break femur. No point in crying out for help as inane film blaring out on TV, so crawl away into kitchen to die.

thirty

SPOUSE ENTERS WAVING LONG-FORGOTTEN box of crackers bought by Tom from Green Light Emporium.

'I found these on top of the wardrobe.'

Children fall on him with glee and rip box apart.

'Ah. Wholemeal pacifist crackers made by hand,' observes Spouse in sardonic tone of which I tire rather easily these days. Whole family grunt and strain but crackers will not split.

'Probably made of recycled carpet,' comments Spouse. Cracker has to be circumcised before, at last, it quietly parts revealing empty cardboard tube.

'Nothing in it!' wails Harriet. 'Snot fair!'

'You can't expect a pacifist cracker to go bang or have anything in it,' shrugs Spouse. 'It's probably a Buddhist statement.'

Wish Tom's crackers would get their act together. Obscurely embarrassed, even though I am the only person who knows Tom bought them.

Further crackers are anatomized and, thank God, reveal paper hats, jokes and knick knacks – including a tape measure with inches on one side and soothsaying epigrams on reverse. Henry measures his head and is informed 'Empty Vessels Make Most Noise.' Well, says Spouse, at least that seems to be working.

Later children watch something violent and deafening on TV whilst we doze over the travel pages. Suddenly Harriet runs in and cries Mummy my knickers smell of Marmite! Inform her that this is simply the human condition. Then she suffers one of those unfortunate random outbursts of innocence which can topple empires.

'Mummy when is Tom coming back to live with us again?'

Spouse looks up from his paper, revealing unusual Alert State, i.e. something approaching consciousness, and enquires Tom Who?

Dive urgently towards sole of shoe and scrape off imaginary piece of Play-Doh.

'You remember,' mumble into my knees, 'that boy – the plumber.' Hope that word *boy* will have subliminal effect suggesting asexuality. 'The plumber chap. He stayed here for a few days whilst his girlfriend had a hysterectomy.' Hope that

mention of girlfriend will safely neutralise any stray frissons, and plunge into gynaecology will send Spouse scuttling back into newspaper.

'Good idea,' grunts Spouse. 'You should've got him to see to the old pipework in his spare time.'

Feel several decades older when time comes for Spouse to return to U.S.A. Deliver children to Lydia Rainge-Roughver for the day whilst I chauffeur Spouse to Heathrow. 'Air hellair Harriet Charlotte's simply dah-ying to show you her new painy.'

Ten minutes towards Heathrow, have to dash back home again as Spouse has left his passport on hall table.

'Freud,' he informs me, 'would say this betrays a subconscious desire to return.' Retort that it betrays a chronic inability to organise his own life.

'Actually,' grins Spouse, 'it betrays a desire to infuriate wife.'

On way down path, hear old van draw up and Tom leaps out. At the sight of him, scarlet horror crawls from my every pore.

'Left a few things here,' says Tom, with airy nod to Spouse. 'I've still got a key – I'll leave it on the hall table.'

Luckily urgent need to catch plane curtails pleasantries. Half an hour later, just as my heartbeat has returned to normal, Spouse says:

'You know, I think that plumber bloke fancies you.'

'What! Never! You should see his girlfriend. She's a cracker.'

'Well, if you feel the slightest desire for a little fling, don't hold back on my account.'

What the hell did he mean by that? I ask myself as he disappears into Departure Lounge.

Drive home to find Tom's sports bag has gone from cupboard under stairs and he has left his front door key on the hall table. Do not need Freud to tell me this betrays a desire not to return.

Feel sick. Sit down and encircle head with soothsaying tape

measure. It says *Think Of Your Faults*. Cannot be Buddhist tape measure surely – Calvinist, more like. Glance at clock and gasp. Must collect children before they are completely gentrified. Would like a bloody good cry but haven't got the time.

thirty-one

SO. TOM DISAPPEARS FROM my life at the very moment when Spouse mysteriously urges me towards extra-marital dalliance. What is Spouse up to in Winnesota? Wonder if he was tempted to tango, whether he would wear a condom. Feel this is unlikely. Spouse famous for his inability to be properly dressed for any occasion.

Wind wuthers round house and strange splintering bump resounds in attic – as of something wooden and vital keeling over. Self-respect, perhaps. Sigh deeply. Were Tom here, he would no doubt vault up there instantly with the elasticity of youth, trainers, and the desire to please. Marvel anew at men's ability to mend machines, hump wardrobes about and climb into attics with every appearance of enjoyment.

Examine if I have any idea who or what Spouse really is, whether I am in any sense married to him and, if so, do I actively desire to remain so? Otherwise –

Interrupted, luckily, by Mrs Twill who informs me the fence has blown down. Wonder if this a symbol of disintegration of the moral order. Mrs Twill laments it would happen while Bernard is in hospital. Express concern, and am informed that Bernard felt twinges round the heart yesterday afternoon and was admitted as a precaution.

Feel twinges round the heart myself, but successfully stifle urge to confide all to Mrs Twill and instead agree with her that men have their uses, that I hope Bernard is back in harness soon, and that I and the children will visit him in hospital forthwith. Taking Henry and Harriet to visit the recently hospitalised could be one solution to the problem of an ageing population.

Next afternoon, spend twenty minutes attempting to find a parking space in hospital car park. By the time I succeed, the children have eaten most of the chocolates and grapes and are well into their twenty-seventh chorus of

'*Neigh. . .bours*
Pick your nose and taste the fla. . .vours.'

Wonder if aforementioned lyric would find a mention in an updated Opie.

Trek through mazes of corridor which smell of wounds, antiseptics and gravy all at once. Feel sudden urge to be sick but manage to distract myself with brief fantasy of Dr. Kildare. Realise I missed this week's LA LAW and curse myself. LA LAW so glossy that it is hard to imagine participants are endowed with pubic hair.

'What do they do with the legs they cut off, here?' asks Henry. 'Do they burn them or bury them? And if they bury them do they get sort of gravestones saying Here Lies Mr Twill's Leg?'

Assure them, unconvincingly perhaps, that Mr Twill's leg is unlikely to be removed as he is in here for his heart.

'I hate this place,' says Harriet. 'It stinks.'

'But Harriet – you were born here!'

Harriet charmed by this news, and points to sign saying *General Manager*.

'Look!' she shouts. 'It says *manger*! Praps this is where Jesus was born, too!'

Eventually find Mr Twill and submit to tirade about Pakistani doctors.

'They're just not like us, Dulcie!' he booms. I cringe.

Actually, it's Twill I feel is Not Like Us Dulcie. Make feeble attempt to query his racist monologue at which he softens.

'Ah!' he concedes, 'Imran Khan! Now there's a tremendous chap!' Cannot but agree.

Emerge depressed into what should be fresh air but turns out to be carbon monoxide and acid rain soup.

Experience strange rogue hope that, when we get home, Tom will be waiting on the doorstep with an enormous bouquet. Alas, only enormous thing awaiting us is a pile of washing up.

Children watch *ET* whilst I attack chores. Wonder what Tom will do next and conclude I have no idea. Spouse even more of a mystery.

Eventually, just as I'm nerving myself up to switch on the Radio 4 News, Harriet rushes in in post-*ET* ecstasy.

'Mummee!' she shouts. 'I want to marry an alien when I grow up!'

'Don't worry, darling,' I reply wearily. 'You will.'

thirty-two

CHILDREN ASLEEP: SETTLE DOWN to an evening's goggling. Cannot face Bonkbuster; am haunted by persistent silence from Tom; queasily aware that children's thank-you letters are unwrit and Christmas decorations unplucked-down. Presumably seven years' bad luck has been notched up in heaven, or wherever Dame Fortune holds her court. Las Vegas, perhaps.

Switch over to ITV and am appalled by sudden vision of Ted Heath, Grocer at last, selling cheese. All the same, heartening to know one can start off as a struggling Prime Minister and eventually rise to the dizzy heights of TV personality. Get up and cut myself large slice of Stilton. Delicious.

On return to TV, am shocked rigid by associated apparition: Ken Livingstone extolling the virtues of Red Leicester. Gasp and choke on Stilton. Where will it all end? Gorby advertising Red Windsor? Or should that be Prince Charles?

Phone rings. Appalled to recognise frosty clang of Great Aunt Elspeth in Medium Dudgeon.

'Is everything all right, Dulcie? I had heard nothing from you, dear. I was worried.'

'Oh yes, well, gosh, I'm terribly sorry –'

Invent series of catastrophes, elevating Harriet's ear infection to crisis precipitating full-scale NATO alert and enquiring if Spouse did not ring to wish her a happy Hogmanay as I clearly remember telling him to. No. Apparently Aunt received no word from Spouse during his entire ten-day sojourn in U.K. Sigh at this criminal omission, and hastily endow him with painful bilious attack lasting several days.

'Dear me,' says Aunt E., 'you have all been in the wars! Did the children get my parcel all right?'

Oh heavens! Intestines knot themselves into tasteful macramé plant-holder – always a symptom of extreme panic. What the hell did Aunt Elspeth give Henry and Harriet this year? Mind goes so blank it cannot remember any of the presents received by H. and H., from anyone.

'Oh they were absolutely thrilled to bits! You really shouldn't have! They were – er – playing with them all day.'

'But I sent them both a W.H.Smith's token.'

Tasteful macramé plant-holder snaps, and pot-plant plummets through pelvic floor.

'Yes. It was extraordinary! Henry made a sort of paper plane thing from his, and Harriet made a magic carpet from hers, and they were, er, flying them up and down the sitting room all day.'

'How very curious, dear.'

'Yes, wasn't it? But how are *you*, Elspeth?'

Aunt Elspeth obligingly rehearses blood-curdling series of ailments starting with Deep Vein in Legs anxiety and culminating with persistent conviction that the top of her head is starting to let in the rain.

'Oh, so's mine! But it's been so stormy this winter! Did you know our fence blew down?'

'Did it? Och, dear, I'm so worried about you and the bairns, all alone.'

Doorbell rings. Excuse myself but Aunt refuses to ring off.

'The doorbell at this time of night? I won't hang up, dear, if you don't mind – just in case.'

Comforting to know that if mass-murderer forces his way in, aged Aunt will bark ferociously at him down the telephone. Probably not murderer, though – just Mrs Twill next door with news of fresh disasters.

But lo! Tom bursts in and before I can utter a syllable, has dragged me into sitting room, pinned me to the sofa, and hissed in tones of appalling clarity:

'You're so sexy! You're so damned sexy! O.K. so you're a total moral coward and unscrupulous and exploitative, but I've decided to give you one last chance because you're so sexy!'

Gesture urgently towards phone. Tom goes pale and freezes in mid-lunge, like youth on Grecian urn. Pick up receiver and brace myself for Caledonian horror. Will tell her it was a Kissogram from Winnesota.

'Hello, Elspeth . . . ?'

'Hello, dear. Everything all right? I'll ring off now if you don't mind. I think I can hear something interesting on the TV. One of those wildlife programmes.'

thirty-three

'AH DECLARE, COUNT AH don't think you've had the oppurtoonity to admire mah prize pumpkins,' simpered Mrs Pershing, glowing, in the steamy Georgia afternoon, above her quivering corsage of Gardenias.

'Indeed not, Madam.' Peveril soon found himself among the matron's extensive hotbeds.

'These,' beamed Mrs Pershing, prodding a swelling pustule with the ibex-horn tip of her parasol, 'are my pride and joy. Tennessee Balls of Fire, Count. See? Aren't they just fat'n'sassy? But ah do like to see a good plump bloom on a fruit. Puts me in mind o'mah young Donna.' Peveril silently inclined his head. He had feared the

conversation would come round to the ripeness of Donna, in time.
'Are you fond of fruit, Count?'

*'Of course. Though on my estates at Yeltsinborg all horticultural
endeavour was left in the hands of my gardener Cherbagov. Ah! How
savagely he would prune the precocious shoots of my Vitatis
Landsbergis!'*

*The sound of girlish laughter echoed through the sweet chestnut
grove, and Donna Pershing and Puce O'Dowd burst with a giggle out
of a thicket of wild tobacco: then, spying Peveril, they pulled up
abruptly, Donna's goggling orbs cast down upon her own almost
dangerous déshabillé; Puce's sparkish gree –*

Wait! What colour are Puçe O'Dowds's eyes for heaven's
sake? Hell! Must trawl through entire second draft of Bonkbuster till I find previous reference to ocular event. Pretty sure
they must be green as Puce is wild heroine, unlike self. Own
eyes have never flashed challengingly except in extremes of
childcare, and even then always require urgent Optrexing
afterwards. Sigh deeply, and pull muscle in lung.

Peveril, despite extensive sentimental education in stews of
St Petersburg, seemingly unable to bed either of these two
tiresome Belles, both, in their different ways, begging for it.
Peveril doomed instead to inspect vegetables or doze on
balconies for weeks on end. Whatever is wrong with the
fellow? . . . Bonkbuster? Unworthy the genre. Alternative
remedy to insomnia, more like.

Feel damp sensation spreading through soul and suspect
leak in spiritual plumbing.

Tom knocks and enters bearing teatray, crumpets, etc.
Deep gratitude whelms up in me, not unaccompanied by
slight misgiving.

'Written to him yet, then?'

'N – not yet.'

'Come on. You're not worthy of all this, Dulcie. Face up to
it. You said yourself you thought he smelt a rat. Put the poor
bastard out of his misery.'

Feel sure that whatever Spouse is up to in Winnesota,

misery is absent from his judiciously austere repertoire of emotions.

Tom takes off my shoe and caresses my foot. Cannot help wishing he would not do this in mid-crumpet.

'Where are the children?'

'They're watching a video. Wildlife thing. Lions tearing wildebeests to bits. You know.'

Encounter first encouraging thought of day: at least I am not required, when hungry, to rush out into street and tear the head off the most fragile-looking of my fellow-creatures.

'I feel pathologically stalled,' I confess. 'In my work, in my life . . . even this crumpet is losing its charm.'

'Sometimes,' says Tom crisply, getting up, but not replacing my shoe, 'you're even more of an adolescent than I am.' And exits, probably miffed that I went off his crumpet.

'Mummy!' Harriet runs in. 'Please can we make a den in your bedroom?'

Pen falls from my nerveless fingers.

'Anything,' I groan. Rest cheek on crumpet. Recall Norman Tebbit's stream of bile towards 'the . . . naive, guilt-ridden, wet, pink orthodoxy of that sunset home of the third-rate minds of that third-rate decade, the 1960s'.

Damp sensation in soul returns. Suspect it is guilt-ridden, wet, pink, orthodoxy. Never one to disobey The Norm. Haunted by conviction that somewhere in the not-too distant future, my bike awaits.

thirty-four

FEEL STRANGE NOSTALGIA FOR good old days of Cold War when nobody dared to lift a finger. Henry resurrects his Action Man doll. Harriet's three Sindies wait patiently on the arm of the sofa ready to entertain him when hostilities are over.

Own dolls used to be babies that said *Mama*. Harriet's dolls would more convincingly enquire *Fancy a nice time dearie?* Back in 1950s, dolls designed to con us into role of Little Mother. Harriet's Sindies, leering in their lurex as she combs their Californian manes, have made of her a Little Madam.

Staggered to see, on *Antiques Roadshow*, eighteenth century doll with slightly chipped nose but still worth £50,000. Fifty grand! You could probably buy a bungalow in Lincolnshire for that.

Action Man performs atrocity upon Sindies causing them to fall into coal-scuttle. Harriet screams, kicks Henry on shin. Henry roars, pulls Harriet's hair. I shriek For God's sake let's have a bit of peace at least here on our own blasted hearthrug. Harriet bursts into outraged tears *Our hearthrug's not blasted!* Not yet, my child. Not yet.

Sometimes wish I was in a bungalow in Lincolnshire, reading *Bleak House*. Alone.

Tom returns from work with *Penne al Pomodoro*, entertains children by speaking in ghostly monotone through length of plastic pipe; baths them – achieving jacuzzi effect by blowing down different length of plastic pipe; and puts them to bed, giving Oscar-winning performance of Burglar Bill with striking impersonations of Bob Hoskins as Burglar Bill and Bette Midler as Burglar Betty.

Something suggests that it is time I threw away the Bulgar Wheat, which has languished unused in its jar for three years. Despite passing qualm about shortages, also throw away Couscous, miscellany of Venomous Beans, Cracked Wheat and Pine Kernels. Sour smell of stagnant cereals pervades kitchen. Too late, realise I could have consigned them to Tom's new improved compost heap. Yes, he has rationalised my rubbish.

Belatedly remember to make coffee – my sole contribution to domestic harmony since he came in through door. Cannot understand why I am becoming so depressed and inert. Only

BBC TV has power to rouse me, with News of Fresh Disasters. Nine O'Clock coming up – rush to gogglebox.

'Hi, they're asleep,' says Tom, coming in and cuddling me in the middle of headlines. Grunt appreciatively. Feel genuine gratitude but do not wish to encourage him towards conversation till after bulletin. Previously thought that the vital classification of humanity was those with a sense of humour and those without. Now realise it is those who talk during the News, and those who preserve a dignified and helpful silence.

'Of course,' says Tom as first report unfolds, 'Nostradamus predicted all this.'

Have become rather cheesed-off with Nostradamus recently and wish urgently to commune uninterruptedly with BBC reporters in sand dunes, who have all become mysteriously glamorous in last few weeks. Perhaps I should get myself a camouflage jacket and a bottle of Sudden Tan. Fear however that bravery cannot be bought over counter in Boots.

'*He will enter: evil, unpleasant, infamous, tyrannizing over Mesopotamia. . . .* Mesopotamia's Iraq, right? Isn't it amazing?'

Nod and fix gaze stubbornly upon Michael Buerk. Tom continues to leaf through battered copy of *Prophecies*.

> '*Sa main derniere par* Alus *sanguinaire,*
> *Ne se pourra par la mer guarentir;*
> *Entre deux fleuves craindre main militaire* –

See, Dulcie? *Alus* could be the Allies, right? In the end he can't protect himself against the bloody Allies. Between two rivers – Iraq again – he will fear the military hand. Incredible, yeah?'

Out of corner of eye, catch sight of advert for GQ – *The Men's Magazine with an I.Q . . . see what it takes to be a real man. Plus the master of serial murder fiction. And the world's deadliest island.*

Suddenly receive blinding flash of insight, switch off telly, hurl Nostradamus into Magazines for Recycling box and crush dear, tender, pacifist, helpful Tom to my bosom. The real man is the one who puts the kids to bed. Stop his mouth with a kiss. The only way, happily, of getting him to shut up.

thirty-five

My dearest husband,

If I may so presume, after having betrayed you, and with a Kapok! Though Cherbagov is an excellent fellow, as I remember your remarking when you first engaged him, on the recommendation of Count Starsky. And indeed I confess 'twas I who pursued him, and for many months he would not look me in the eye, but fixed his powerful gaze instead upon the turnips. Indeed not till the fatal Feast of St Karvol – but I digress.

Alas, dear Peveril! How I do repent me of my rash elopement, now! Snow lies thick upon the Regenwald. I have only a rancid wolfskin to protect me, and an old woodpecker's nest from which to contrive a humble soup. Cherbagov is so much preoccupied with the hostilities, that I often pass entire days without a salutation from any living creature, save my tame Transylvanian swine Dymbulbi. The expression of innocent intelligence in this creature's eyes! – But I digress.

But perhaps you have not heard of the unrest. A passing Kapok conveyed to me a rumour that you are gone to America, to visit the Pershings I presume. O dear Peveril, cannot you convey me thither, I beg? For the Smurfs have invaded Arcadia, the Bruts and Tabacs are revolting, and we heard this week the appalling news that Milcbottyl has fallen. Poor Cherbagov is assailed also with bodily ills – he has the Baltics – and I am sure his hair-shirt and drawers do naught but aggravate the condition.

I do not deserve to be received as your wife, but should you require a willing serf to anoint your top-boots with bear grease and lay out your boned Prussian underweskit, do not hesitate to summon

Your most devoted and penitent,
Charlotte Beaminster.

I no longer feel entitled to call myself a de la Palmas de Santa Cruz.

Pray write to me care of the schoolmaster at Triominic.

Peveril uttered a light but savage laugh, and tossed the letter onto the glowing coals upon which several of Mrs Pershing's slaves were basting a Roebuck.

'Bad news, Count?' drawled Puce O'Dowd, sauntering up to him with a half-gnawed spare rib dangling from her wicked little fingers, which glistened tantalisingly with the grease. 'Don't spoil the picnic with one of your Slavic sulks. Ah declare, ah ain't seen you smile above once since I first set eyes on you at that hop at Marlon County.'

Peveril sighed.

'Come!' whispered Puce, an alarming flash of mischief in her eye. 'Come and gnaw mah spare rib in the summerhouse down by the creek! Nobody's lookin' – they're all knee deep in old Ma Pershing's Hominy'n'Beans Bazookas.'

And she boldly seized his hand and led him away through the burgeoning groves of the Cottonbud.

'Mummeeee! Can't *breathe!*' Harriet storms in wearing a pale green moustache. No hankies left so hastily remove it with the hem of my skirt – already, thank God, adorned with axle grease and tomato soup upon a most helpful tropical print. 'Want Sinex! *Now!*'

It says on the bottle *For children over six years* but she will be, next month, and besides, her reading age is eight.

Must remember to write to what's her name about Harriet's reading age so she can boast about it at the w.i. Good Heavens! Have forgotten name of Great Aunt! Not a good augury for my own mental capacity when – and if – I too attain that lofty status. But perhaps by then Vicks will be marketing helpful little inhalers to decongest the ancient brain: Senex.

Cringe slightly at sound of Tom's key in front door. All too aware that he will have found some new prediction from Nostradamus to enliven our evening – yesterday it was fire, blood, plagues and death hidden in flying globes. No doubt also I shall once more be interrogated along the lines of *have you written to him yet?* Though perhaps Nostradamus will have predicted my failure in this respect and spare us the usual tedious preamble to the vegetarian sausages, Mung beans and hummus which I fear will be our destiny tonight.

thirty-six

WOKEN UP IN MIDDLE of night by strange rhythmical whistling. Furtive signals of gang of burglars surrounding house? Last gasp of antiquated central heating system? Tom has gone to stay with his sister for a couple of days and therefore I must deal with sinister whistling alone. Then realise it is emanating from my own nose. Probably side-effect of having paid through it so often recently.

Since I am awake, it seems only human to start worrying about the war. I am, of course, right behind our lads and lasses in the Gulf, especially Mrs Body's nephew Andy who is a Desert Rat, or, according to Henry, a Gerbil. I am also right behind the poor Iraqis and appalled that I have helped to pay for some of the bombs raining down on them. I suppose you could say I was lying on the fence.

But when the chips are down, I stand shoulder to shoulder with the dear Beast of Bolsover and Tony Benn, who will always be a young firebrand in my eyes. Although firebrand perhaps not a suitable soubriquet in present circumstances. A young fire extinguisher? Lacks the éclat, somehow. And as for Edward Heath: why did we have no inkling that he was going to turn out to be wonderful? He is blossoming now, all over the place, like bamboo.

Drift into uneasy sleep, and dream that I am directing a production of *A Midsummer Night's Dream* in which Oberon is played by Colin Powell, Puck by Peter de la Billiere, Quince by Douglas Hogg, and Bottom by Norman Schwarzkopf. Kate Adie, with a stern flash of pearl, complains that the nine men's morris is filled up with mud.

Awake to discover this is not *A Midsummer Night's Dream* but the same old Midwinter Nightmare. Tempted to get up and make tea but at 4 a.m. this seems a little too apocalyptic even for these days.

Phone Spouse as it is probably evening in Winnesota. He sounds faintly annoyed by my interruption and in the background I can hear the TV roaring away with some kind of American sporting event, possibly the War. Make despairing references thereto which Spouse ignores.

'If only we could settle it all with a game of cricket,' I sigh. 'Such a shame the Iraqis can't play.'

'Well, at the moment, nor can we,' observes Spouse acidly.

Recount my dream about Schwarzkopf as Bottom but can tell that its wondrous, revelatory quality is escaping him. Apologise and hang up, with a sigh, though Spouse's dry refusal to be agitated even by Third World War is faintly comforting.

Drift back to sleep and dream that the war has become a Test Match with Brian Johnson and Trevor Bailey commentating. Saddam is a fast bowler – a sort of Fred Trueman on speed, and Botham (my subconscious enjoys a better class of selector) hits Saddam all over the ground like a Patriot missile launcher made flesh. Awoken in middle of Brian Johnson's first chocolate cake by strange rhythmical whistling sound.

Sit up in bed and reach for exercise book.

The summer house was deserted. Puce O'Dowd stepped boldly in, and Peveril followed, out of curiosity, perhaps. The peeling boards of the simple wooden ceiling flickered with reflected light from the creek. A faded old daybed, a couple of basket chairs, a scrap of cotton rug on the bare planked floor. . . . Peveril was satisfied by the reflection that his own summerhouse at Lake Virol was much more sumptuously appointed.

'Ah'll jus' draw th'blinds,' breathed Puce O'Dowd, and with a

sinuous movement of her lithe young shoulders, a seductive dimness fell on Peveril's strangely burning orbs. She turned to face him, and threw herself tauntingly on the daybed, in the provocative posture Peveril had admired in the portrait of La Comtesse de Benaud by David – or was it Goya? – at the Hermitage.

'Well, Count,' purred Puce, and her voice rubbed up against his eardrum like a cat against a dustbin, 'folks say you're a'goin' to marry Donna Pershing.'

'Madam,' Peveril informed her with a rapidly-stiffening spine, 'I am married already.'

thirty-seven

PEVERIL GARGLED MOODILY WITH Mint Julep. The encounter with Puce O'Dowd in the summerhouse had left a bitter taste in his mouth. Her habit of chewing tobacco was unfortunate.

'Dmitri!' he called. 'Another Mint Julep!'

Dmitri shuffled in, his thick peasant hair tumbled about like a cornfield in which peasants had misbehaved en masse.

'You are unkempt,' observed Peveril crisply. 'I hope you are not keeping lewd company.'

Dmitri paused at the door and spat accurately into a pot of Yucca.

'I wouldn't touch them nasty loose trollops with a hayfork,' he sneered. 'Who knows where they've been?'

The shadow of a qualm scudded across Peveril's soul. He wouldn't have touched Puce either, but the obligations of a gentleman . . . he sighed. He had often noticed how Dmitri in his serfdom seemed strangely more free than his master, trussed up with the etiquette of civilisation.

He longed to expel the taste of Puce. The memory of Charlotte's sweet breath drifted down the corridors of his memory. He picked up his antelope horn travelling pen:

My dear Charlotte,

I acknowledge your salutations and pity your distress, but circumstances forbid my summoning you here to Marlon County. For the present therefore I can only advise you to remain in what are no doubt the discomforts of the Regenwald. I have camped there often on manoeuvres and advise you to avoid the Dewberry as it can cause the most exquisite cramps.

As for Cherbagov's unfortunate affliction, pray inform him that the very worst course, with the Baltics, is to keep scratching them, which will only inflame them the more. Only leave them alone and they will drop off harmlessly in time. Though why I should offer this helpful counsel to the man who stole my wife is paradoxical. Since he is not a gentleman I may not challenge him, but I do feel a strange tremor of sympathy for the lout – as indeed I would for any fellow burdened with your care, my sweet.

No doubt we shall meet again in time. I think of you often: sometimes with fondness, sometimes with fury, but increasingly, thank G –, with philosophical resignation.

> *Cordially,*
> *Peveril St Canonicorum de las Palmas de Santa Cruz.*

Attend Harriet's school dinner (parents welcome on Fridays). Admire small girl sitting next to Harriet with long silky eyelashes and air of Botticelli angel. Harriet, by comparison, resembles small cross-eyed carnivorous monkey. What a piece of work is man, et cetera, in his something or other how like an ape, but on the other hand, in his whossname how like an angel.

Must re-read Shakespeare and perhaps steal one of his plots and recycle it into Bonkbuster, which appears totally stalled and lacking in chutzpah. Cravenly averted my eyes from Peveril's collision with Puce in the summerhouse when I knew full well 'twas my duty to be there recording every rip and groan.

School dinner delicious: choice of three main courses and several veg., plus delicious steamed pud and custard. Stomach feels outraged, like handbag into which six library books and three pounds of plums have been inconsiderately thrust.

After coffee with other Mums, find Harriet crying in cloak-room with angelic child who insists she was only joking.

'She says she hates me!' sobs Harriet. 'And she says she's going to kill my Mummy!'

Ask angelic child whether Thursday would be convenient, at which she also bursts into tears and runs off.

'You fool, Mummy!' snaps Harriet. 'You shouldn't have said that!'

On way home reflect that I have never known what to say to children and that I often feel like nineteenth century gentleman perplexed by necessity of co-existing with loutish multitude. No wonder there are wars.

Mind you, in present international situation, am haunted by the conviction that the gentlemen and angels are fled, and we are all louts together, struggling in a bag, hanging on the kitchen door of God. Have been reading too many fairy tales recently, but who can blame me?

thirty-eight

HARRIET SUFFERS FRESH OUTBREAK of burglarphobia and announces that she had a dream in which a fierce man in a balaclava burst through the back door with an axe. Only too aware that our back door could be penetrated by a gentle man in a Panama with a teaspoon. Henry reminds me that there is a large bolt lying unused in one of the cupboards in the Futility Room, bought two years ago for this very back door and, due to Spouse's graceful inertia, never fixed.

'I'll get Tom to put it on tonight when he gets home.'

'I can do it, Mum!' Henry seizes screwdriver with frighten-ing fervour. Tools, weapons, me Tarzan, me wield 'em.

'We'll *all* do it!' I insist quickly, heart sinking at memory of previous forays into carpentry.

'Don't *want* to do it!' screams Harriet. 'Want to play with Sindies!'

'It would do you good to learn how to fix bolts on, my girl! That's what was wrong with my education – not enough Meccano, too many bloody dolls!'

Harriet bursts into tears and runs off. Henry and I wrestle fruitlessly with bolt and screws till, at height of struggle, I cry *Please, please, God: help us fix this sodding door.* Henry looks gravely at me and says I don't think He approves of swearing Mummy. Eventually surrender, marvelling that Joseph, when burdened with outrageous demands of carpentry, could also take on responsibility for nurturing Messiah.

Harriet runs in and hits me on the head with a handcrafted Himalayan nose-flute, which breaks. Reflect – somewhat dizzily – that despite doll-centred education, I cannot deal with people either.

Remonstrate with her about violence against the person, and reverence due to artefacts from Developing World, especially those donated by Aunt Elspeth.

Wonder if flute can be mended by Tom as after all, it is in a sense a fragment of Buddhist plumbing. Wish he would come home. Feel I have been unduly irritable towards him recently but hope I can blame it on the war. Resolve to be more tender and considerate towards my loved ones. Keep the home fires burning, etc.

Spouse has not rung for nearly a week. Wonder, perhaps with guilty hope, whether he has been crowbarred into transatlantic dalliance with Sally or perhaps succumbed to a Sophomore. O Tempora! O Sophomores!

Make unnecessarily long petrol-consuming journey past Tesco's to patronise Islamic grocery store on far side of town. Harriet grumbles that there are no Fiendish Feet yoghurts and Henry comments loudly that the apples are all going wrinkly. Insist that the wrinkliest are the sweetest when it comes to apples and women, and buy three pounds of them. Cannot get a smile out of tired woman on till. Feel that trip did not contribute much to Christian-Islamic relations.

Back home, give children popular supper of cheese and ketchup sandwiches made of pulpy, white bread. Tom rings to say he will be late and, whilst I am on the phone, Henry and Harriet arrange themselves in post-massacre tableau, using remaining half-pint of ketchup.

'That's not in a very good taste,' I comment, wearily opening new pack of Jeycloths.

'Yes it is, Mummy! It tastes *very* good!'

Children lick each other's wounds. Stare despairingly into mug of decaffeinated Earl Grey.

When children are in bed, prepare curry and put on scarlet silk camisole against Tom's return. He is somewhat revived by the spices but, upon retiring to the boudoir, informs me there is no need to tart myself up for him.

'I'm not so much turned on by your bum and stuff,' he says, 'as by your spiritual resonance.'

At these words, my own libido wilts. Feel sorry for my bum, and remind Tom that religion has got us into another fine mess internationally, and I'd rather it was left out of the bedroom if he didn't mind. Tom retorts that Gulf War nothing to do with religion, more a chance for macho man to test his nice new hardware.

Equally repelled by the idea of Holy War and Smart Bombs. Fall asleep haunted by conviction that there is no room for me in a world of Mecca versus Meccano.

thirty-nine

PEVERIL RAN AN ELEGANT *finger impatiently up and down the gleaming mahogany . . .*

The gleaming mahogany what? Side table at steamy Southern buffet? Piano at which Donna Pershing is conducting quivering search for Lost Chord? Gleaming mahogany

. . . baseball bat? Dazed by huge range of possible experiences awaiting Peveril, and bewildered by Peveril's unvarying disinclination thereto.

Eye wanders fatally from authorial duties towards Next catalogue. Ruefully admire elegant fawn tie-front trousers, which I ordered recklessly a month ago and are still hanging unworn in the wardrobe because they make me look fat. Wonder why they do not make the girl in the Next catalogue look fat. Perhaps because she isn't.

Turn to men's underwear section and for some reason start to feel hot. Marvel how they manage to get away with it. Ah!

Peveril ran an elegant finger impatiently up and down the gleaming mahogany spine of his erstwhile-clothed serf Dmitri. 'To think,' he mused, 'of the tedious evenings I have spent . . .'

'Mummeee! You know that peel–off children's nail varnish, well as it's peel–off can I paint the walls with it?'
'Er . . . yes dear. Now go away, Mummy's working.'

'. . . tossing in my solitary cabin on the transatlantic crossing, idling away my hours at sweaty hops, when all the time. . . '

Imagine TV version with Jeremy Irons as Peveril and Anthony Andrews as Dmitri, slowly divesting themselves of chic nineteenth century coms by Next.

'Harriet's made a mess!' Henry puts his holier-than-thou head prefect's face round the door. Sigh and request him to escort me thither.

In midst of fawn sitting-room carpet is huge pink stain as if My Little Phoney has had fatal haemorrhage – which, alas, unlikely. Why ever did I buy that carpet? Fawn a dreadful colour, and the stains will be there for ever.

'You told me I could!' screams Harriet in ecstasy of guilt. Gnash teeth and experience exquisite spear of pain. Recollect that I skipped last dental appointment and rush to phone. We've just had a cancellation for this afternoon, says the nice receptionist. Can you make 2.30?

Dash upstairs and clean teeth properly for the first time in ten months – i.e. since last dental appointment. Astonished gums bleed in indignation. Realise I smell. Must change clothes. Only fair to dentist – charming young man who never hurts.

Rip off smelly tracksuit and don new Next fawn tie-front trousers and immaculate white blouse. Look fat but smell clean. Have last frenzied pee and rise to discover I have peed comprehensively all over one of the foolish dangling ties. Consign garment to laundry basket after approximately forty-five seconds wear. Fawn most unflattering colour in any case and the stains will be there for ever.

In car on way to dentist recall that Fawn is also a name, as in Fawn Hall, Oliver North's Sindian Personal Assistant, the one who was such a dab hand with the shredder. Fawn Hall sounds monumental, somehow – like an institution. Perhaps the people who issue Court Circulars.

Children bicker in back seat over calculator – educational toy designed to stimulate their numeracy. Harriet asks me what is 173 plus 56. Inform her I am above such things.

On dentist's couch, realise that though immensely relieved the war is over, I do miss General Schwarzkopf – or Blackhead, as Tom refers to him, no doubt out of youthful pique and jealousy. Surely the cuddly toy manufacturers will be on to Stormin' Norman. He is after all essentially a Gonk with balls.

Will not miss scenes of desert on TV, however. Endless vistas of fawn. Sort of macro–sitting room carpet. And the stains will be there for ever.

forty

'I HATE MUMMY. SHE is a Big Fat Poo Poo.' Bright red graffiti appears in the bathroom. Glad there are no spelling mistakes, though half the letters are back to front. Not bothered by *hate*:

a fleeting mood of natural rebellion. *Big* is O.K. as I am twice Harriet's size. Rather hurt, however, by *fat*.

Examine myself in the brief privacy of the bathroom mirror and conclude that I have put on half a stone during Lent. If indeed that was Lent which just whizzed by. Useless modern diaries no longer register religious festivities. Recall with a fond smile old Cambridge diary, especially: Jan 1st, Circumcision. Library Closed.

Fat, eh? Attempt to burn off two thousand calories by scrubbing ineffectually at graffiti with Ecover Cream Cleaner. Graffiti merely fades from the livid to the ruddy – Livingstone to Ruddock, as it were. Recoil at possibility of Harriet's graffiti being last relic of twentieth century civilisation, should our bathroom at 196 Cranford Gardens escape by some fluke the devouring hand of time like a Lascaux cave. Would not wish to go down in post-history as a Big Fat Poo Poo, but perhaps Venus of Willendorf had same fear, in vain.

Prise Harriet away from Pink Panther video and confront her with her crime, at which she throws massive guilt tantrum, almost worse than her habitual tyrannous indignation. Had planned to issue series of sanctions, including no pocket money for three weeks and no felt-tip pen ever again, but am so battered by her emotional tempest that I find myself offering her not only placatory Creme Egg but even a Trip to the Fair. Hell, somebody's got to be a wimp now George Bush is no longer available.

Insist we wait for Tom to come home so he can accompany us. Tom leaps at suggestion of Fair rather like legendary dog, in contrast to Spouse who would have said, 'None but the Brave deserves the Fair,' and retired into Romanticism in National Context.

As usual, initial sight of Fair with music, lights, etc., brings tears of sentimentality to my eyes, but closer inspection produces wave of horror. Tom takes Henry on monstrous aerial wheel to which helpless victims are strapped – in contravention, one suspects, of Geneva Convention. I accompany Harriet into a giant teacup which promises gentler pleasures.

Once the teacup begins to whirl, however, the notion of gentler pleasures is exposed as a craven delusion. Harriet screams in ecstasy. I grit my teeth and expect every moment my tits to fly off in different directions, or at least my last meal to reappear all over my daughter's face. That unpleasant medical phrase 'the brain stem' appears in my mind, sounding horribly fragile.

Eventually the mad cartwheeling of the universe comes to an end (though not, alas, in any apocalyptic sense) and I numbly climb off. We discover Henry and Tom eating hamburgers and suddenly the way Tom smacks his lips when eating begins to irritate me, though, aeons ago, when I first noticed it, I was sure it never would.

Harriet and I visit abysmal Ladies Loo with even worse graffiti. Harriet stares at the wall.

'Mummy!' she booms, 'What's a wanker?'

'Er, I don't know darling. Something to do with plumbing I think.'

'Is Tom a wanker too, then?'

'Certainly not!'

Much later, after News at Ten, Tom yawns and musses my hair, and says for fifth time this week, 'Must go to the Ba'athroom and have shi'ite.'

Smile wanly, and enjoy brief sweetness of solitude. Wonder how soon he too will notice that the writing is on the wall.

forty-one

'MUMMY! WHY'S IT CALLED Good Friday?'

Ransack memory for any Easter relics, but find only Paschal Lambert Simnel, Orthodox Russian incensed by Fabergé egg . . . (must reactivate Bonkbuster and introduce generous pinch of sex and violence thereto) . . . chic bonnets, Bugs Bunny, *Urbi et Orbi ab Ovo*, John Donne Riding Westward (luckily before the advent of British Rail Leaf Tea) and Pope on Balcony fluttering and dancing in the breeze. Not so much stream of consciousness: more drip of oblivion.

Hope children will not ask questions about crucifixion. Christianity O.K. at Christmas with baby, donkeys, etc., but at Easter prefer multicultural detour, preferably via Buddhist – or is it Hindu – heaven complete with wine, houris, etc.

'It's called Good Friday because all children are supposed to be extra good.'

'Ugh!' comments Harriet. 'When's Bad Friday then?'

'Waal Count, how're we-all goin' fer to celebrate Mardi Gras?' drawled Puce O'Dowd, gnawing the butt of a Havana cigar. The dark stain of her saliva upon the weed provoked a shudder of distaste in Peveril. Greasy Tuesday. The smell of barbecued bisonburgers drifted through the grove of Missouri Boldwoods and mingled unappetisingly with the sickly whiff of the new hairoil Dmitri had persuaded him to try: Savannah Stephanotis.

Peveril averted his mental gaze from Mardi Gras and looked ahead to Easter. An image from long ago flashed upon his inward eye: Charlotte in a witty little Easter bonnet of Prussian blue crêpe de Chine and ostrich feathers, flirting with Count Eztragen at one of the Czar's garden parties after the usual orgy of incense and bawling at the church of St Mikhail Ignatieff.

If only she could have confined her flirtations to the nobility! His own present skirmish with the loutish Dmitri was no more than a seigneurial duty, and a wearisome one at that, but for her to abandon the matrimonial bed, despite its acres of crackling Chinese chintz and Transylvanian tassels, and flee to a rude hovel in the Regenwald with the preposterous Cherbagov! Why, the fellow was not only subversive but bald! And a good head shorter than myself, thought Peveril, extending his neck heavenward with an aristocratic shudder. How fortunate, he mused, that my birth and education have equipped me with such a useful variety of sigh and shudder. However do the common people manage without them?

May Cherbagov's fortunes be dashed – his cogitations grew vengeful – by a fellow with a lot more hair. May his star be

*comprehensively blasted as he has blasted mine. Then Peveril offered
up one of his most plangent fin-de-siècle sighs. Spring may have come
to the Northern portion of the terraqueous globe, but for him, perhaps
for his whole class, there would be no renewal.*

Renewal! – Oh Lord – *Library books!* Have already received
brusque postcard from Rusbridge Library and fear am now
due for ultimate sanction. Perhaps of a literary nature. Rough
music, maybe. Though rough music administered by librarians perhaps not so bad after all. Surely only mezzo-forte at
worst.

Walk in garden with children who are already greedily
looking for hidden eggs though I have not even bought any
yet. Harriet enquires why are daffodils yellow? Struggle with
Darwinian intricacies for a while before resorting to *because
God painted them yellow for fun.* Harriet asks where the world
came from and Henry informs her a BIG BANG, giving rise to
maternal headache. Harriet asks who was Jesus's Daddy really.
Refer her to the Bishop of Durham. Harriet says Mummy
when it says Jesus rose again does that mean like Superman?
Er, yes darling that's it exactly.

Deep fatigue sets in. Return to house, flop onto sofa and
activate Superman video as quasi-religious experience. Dead
give away of divinity, that rising again business. Completely
beyond my mortal strength to rise once, let alone twice.
Doubt if I shall even be able to get off sofa without the addition
of stiffly-beaten egg whites. Wonder why no spring in my
step. Suspect Oestrogen – or perhaps Easteragain – deficiency.

forty-two

LIGHT AT END OF tunnel visible: Easter holidays draw to a
close. However, Spouse has not phoned for ten days. Am
thinking of serving him with paternity suit. Tom preoccupied

with installation of jacuzzi for Swindon software magnate. Still not sure what software is, or jacuzzi for that matter. Perhaps it is time to order my Lisle stockings and Yorkshire terrier.

Easter hols incomplete without outing, insist children. Suggest nearby National Trust manor house. Children revile vernacular architecture and demand sea. Heart sinks twenty fathoms but reconcile myself to driving to Dorset coast along thronged and irritable 'A' roads.

Though it is only day trip, Harriet insists on taking teddy, goat, tiger, monkey puppet etc., till departing car resembles Ark. Henry demands surfboard – evidently corrupted by aftershave ads. After five mins, still on outskirts of Rusbridge, Harriet enquires urgently Are we nearly there yet I've got a tummyache.

Stop at handsome market town for coffee, scones and Coke floats. Spy Start-rite sign and drag children thither as Harriet has narrow and difficult feet. Harriet insists she wants pink patent court shoes with high heels. Stern shoeshop matriarch offers only pair in stock in Harriet's size: they resemble Victorian corrective shoe for fey foot-fetishist. Harriet scowls. Matriarch scowls too, and doubts that Harriet will ever fill them. Both children scream unsuccessfully for Teenage Mutant Wellies.

Three miles into magical Dorset countryside, have collected my usual retinue of impatient and flashing Transit van, Escorts, etc. Cannot help driving even more slowly than usual as am stuck behind cement lorry and am much too scared to overtake. At times cement lorry pauses to graze from passing verges. Harriet says she feels sick.

Nonsense, I say, you're never sick. Strange choking sounds break out behind me.

'Harriet's been *sick*,' Henry informs me in aggrieved tone. Cannot stop because of incessant pursuit of Transit van. Sick transit Gloria Mundi.

Oh God, says Harriet, I've been sick all over my monkey and I wish I'd never been born.

At length I spy a layby (what Great Aunt Elspeth sometimes refers to as 'a layabout') at which I am able to discover that Harriet has also been sick over tiger and bear but mostly new shoes. Stern shoeshop matriarch quite wrong in her prediction that Harriet would never be able to fill them. Clean her up, in absence of in-car tissues and Wet Ones, with towel which had been intended for post-bathing ministrations.

Drive even more slowly onward to coast hoping for chemist's stocked with Junior Kwells. Harriet sounds more cheerful and remarks that you could tell the sick had been a scone once. I request that she will say no more about it, though aware I am offering the shudder of ancient superstition to her calm scientific scrutiny of the natural world.

Decide it is time to count blessings: not emotionally involved with member of Royal family, not allergic to dust, etc. Coast down scenic hill, probably riddled with pagan overtones, and enter small town. Sun comes out. Leaves unfurl. Blossom shimmers. Spring uncoils. Light at end of tunnel almost palpable.

Then – whoa! Handsome but unsmiling policeman steps out from side of road and flags me down. Stop, with complacent desire to assist constabulary in any project they may be pursuing: Dorset drug-smuggling, old Blue Vinny cheese-forging, Satanic abuse in Cerne Abbas, whatever. Policeman points out that this is built-up area. Blithely concur. Informs me I was doing 43.07 m.p.h. and demonstrates same on strange calculator-like machine, which Henry instantly covets. Courteously requests licence and announces his intention of awarding me a fixed penalty. Express gratitude, though not entirely sure if appropriate, and murmur something about child having been sick. Policeman civil and sympathetic but goes on inexorably filling in horrid yellow form.

Harriet wails Oh are you going to prison Mummy? Reply Alas, alas my child, but no. I fear I shall have to try a little harder.

Policeman remains tight-lipped. As usual, light at end of tunnel has turned out to be bottomless Black Hole.

forty-three

'MUMMY! JOSEPH WAS GOD wasn't he because he was Jesus's father?'

'Er . . . no, darling, um . . . some people say God was Jesus's father but Joseph sort of looked after him.'

'When God was away? Like Tom looks after us?'

Deliver both children to school and on way home endure series of theological parallels. Diverted by idea of Spouse as God the Father, mysteriously absent. Joseph no doubt worth his weight in gold. Bet Mary didn't have to wait three years for her shelves to be put up. Tom also a pearl. Has put up shelves, etc. But yet –

I do not like 'but yet'. He cooks, he shops, he plays with the children, he beats as he sweeps as he cleans, he is always so anxious to please. But yet my perverse soul begins to shrink from this almost strident anxiety to please. Last Sunday at 4 p.m. when he suggested, with shining eyes, that he should whip up some Welsh cakes, why was I reminded for one fatal second, of a Springer spaniel?

And why, despite their many virtues, have spaniels never excited my wholehearted admiration?

Is it the awful white drooping disc above their melting brown eyes, which begs you not to kick them? Their soulful need? Their way of following you around the kitchen and putting their arms around you when you desired nothing more than a solitary moment of blank nose-picking by the microwave? Pawing and fawning. Ah me. Things have not just gone off the boil, alas. Poor Tom's a-cold.

And yet, I muse – turning right into Cranford Gardens with a panache foolhardy in one whose driving licence is already in the hands of the Dorset constabulary – and yet God knows I do not urgently crave the return of Spouse with his crocodilian habits. The hours of cold-blooded inertia punctuated by the occasional snap.

Is mankind, I ask myself desperately, braking too hard as I pass Bernard and Audrey Twill's immaculate front gate; is mankind – and by that I mean the male sort – nothing more than a zoo? Would Spouse and Tom both be happier in a wildlife park? Would I be happier if all I had to do was crawl by in the Volvo now and again and throw them a bun?

Engage reverse – literally, for a start – and attempt to park. Somehow my tail end lurches into the gleaming snout of Bernard Twill's chic new Peugeot with sickening bang. Burst into tears: tears about cars, about men . . . Bernard, ageing loyal labrador to his whiskers, waddles out in dismay. Dread I will provoke another of his heart attacks, but my tears excite his chivalrous nonchalance and reassuring faith in A.A. insurance scheme to cure all ills.

Limp indoors already totally exhausted at only 9.30 a.m. Pick up post, carry it to sofa and slump thereon. Close eyes and issue prayer to God, Aphrodite, Shiva, the A.A. – anyone – to sort out my life before . . . well, before the end of the U.S. academic year, when presumably Spouse will return expecting to bask and snap as before. Endure brief wildlife hallucination of bloody encounter between crocodile and spaniel, complete with breathless commentary by David Attenborough. Oh why could I not have married *him*?

Banish vision of Darwinian struggle between Spouse and Lover, and open first envelope from – amazing co-incidence – the A.A.

'A.A. Insurance – for your Spouse. The A.A. Funeral Expenses Plan.'

Hastily retract prayer for divine assistance, screw up letter and hurl across room. Surely Spouse is entitled to a little more basking before he is finally translated into handbags – the sort that close with a satisfying snap. Enjoy moment of complacent pride that I have never bought anything made of crocodile. Or husband for that matter.

Sigh. Seems ages since I heard a really good sneer. Perhaps that's what I need. Or more time to myself. Yawn, stretch, and enjoy silence, punctuated only by distant sounds of

Bernard mowing and Audrey mopping. Then dammit, typical, etc., etc., phone rings. It is Tom.

'Listen, Dulcie – the way things are going here, I could nip home for a little lunch with you around one. What say?'

forty-four

'LISTEN TO THIS, DULCIE: *"Nudz affamez de froit, soif soy bander,/ Les monts passer commettent grand esclandre."* Naked, starving with cold and thirst, they band together to cross the mountains causing a great scandal.'

Once more Nostradamus has Tom in his grip, perhaps because Dog is staying the night en route for magical Montgomeryshire where he is to help found a meditation and healing centre at a place composed entirely of Ls and Gs. He is to be the resident soothsayer, cultivating his organic Tarots.

'You know,' whispers Tom reverently whilst Dog is on one of his interminable visits to the loo, 'I think Dog is a bit like Coleridge – without the genius, of course.'

It seems to be a case of Love Me, Love My Dog. Suppose I should be grateful for small mercies, though. It could be worse: he could be like Wordsworth without the genius.

'If Kurdistan was full of oil,' Dog bursts in again, full of revelations nurtured in the privy, 'the place would be swarming with bloody Americans, right?'

Wish I had hot dinner – or Kurds 100,000 hot dinners – for every time I have heard this sentiment during the past fortnight.

'Mummy!' Harriet whispers in my ear, 'that man said *bloody*.'

'Too right!' Tom leaps into the saddle of his pacifist high horse. 'Like, it's a massacre. But, you know, the U.S. have always been *totally* hypocritical in their foreign policy.'

'Yeah. It stinks. Imperialism all over again, right? We've got our rocket launchers, we've got our Stealth Bombers, we've got the U.S. marines. . . .'

'I'm going to be a paratrooper when I grow up,' says Henry helpfully.

'No you're not, Henry, that's crap. You're going to be an organic farmer, mate!'

'No I'm not! I want to be a par –'

'An' of course if you want any of the hardware, Mr Third World despot, well, great, we can do you a special deal, $5 off for bulk buys and no questions asked about what you do with your minorities.'

Though I deplore the way my children interrupt grown ups, I also somehow almost deplore the way grown ups occasionally interrupt my children.

'Swords into ploughshares, mate, it's the only way.'

'Yeah. Too right. Sod Trident. Sod Polaris. Sod the Bomb. Chuck the lot into the sea.'

Dog makes expansive gesture narrowly avoiding spaghetti-jar. Forbear to point out that Trident and Polaris are in the sea already, so chucking unnecessary. Also have reservations about irresponsibility of act *vis-à-vis* marine ecology.

'Mummy! What does "Sod Polaris" mean?'

'Just a minute, darling – Hang on a minute, Tom! Suppose Saddam Hussein – or somebody like him – turned up at Rusbridge Primary School –'

Both young men swivel astonished gaze on me. Feel hot under collar. First menopausal flush, perhaps? Or time I cast a clout – in the purely sartorial sense?

'I mean, I'd like to think someone was going to stop him marching my kids off to the gas chambers. Preferably someone like Norman Schwarzkopf – big, fierce and fully armed.'

Tom turns to Dog.

'Dulcie's got the hots for Stormin' Norman, 'cos she's got this secret desire to be dominated by a big bit of rough stuff.'

Dog fixes me for an instant with his terrible seer's glare.

'Dulcie,' he intones, 'I get a strong feeling you're repressing negative feelings, right? That can do, like, untold psychic damage. You gotta, like, well, blow all that stuff away till you're pure like a meadow flower again.'

Feel strange pang of longing for Spouse. When he was here in the good old days it was me who was the radical.

Men resume their dialogue about U.S. foreign policy being no more than a desire to kick ass.

'Mummy! What does "kick ass" mean?'

Heroically suppress desire to demonstrate the process.

forty-five

RECEIVE INVITATION TO ADDRESS Cambridge Union. Feel sick. Debate is to be light-hearted, viz: 'This House Would Rather Flop Down in front of the TV than Get Sweaty on the Sports Field.' All the same, as dreaded date approaches, feel sicker. Unfortunately not sick enough to cancel. Find suppurating old carrot in fridge like some dreadful illustration from medical textbook. Devour it, hoping for spectacular food poisoning. Feel much better.

In the absence of sickness, fall back on the children (not nearly heavily enough and not nearly often enough, but that's another story).

'I can't possibly go all the way to Cambridge!' I whine to Tom, as if this were the fourteenth century and only transport available an undernourished pack horse. 'Who's going to look after the children?'

'Me, of course!' says Tom with one of his most irritating grins. 'We'll have a great time. We'll do all the things they're not allowed to do when you're there.'

Uneasily aware that there is virtually nothing the children aren't allowed to do when I'm there, and that this falls short of the desirable canons of child-rearing.

Urge Tom to immobilise children safely in front of TV and on no account to attempt sweaty exertions outdoors, which as every mother knows, can only lead to tears.

Have spent every spare moment of last five and a half weeks wondering what on earth I shall find to wear. Letter from President informs me dress is 'mildly formal'. What a cop-out. 'Formal' a concession to stuffy establishment. 'Mildly' a concession to liberal déshabillé. Would have preferred 'severely informal'. Then could have worn black patent basque and mini skirt bought in 1971. Still, perhaps better not. Would have resembled something put out for dustmen in black plastic sack.

Mildly formal . . . decide on funeral suit before recalling at last minute it can lead, at moments of extreme emotion, to black armpits. Remember brief Bubonic Plague panic after Uncle Arthur's interment, or as Aunt Edith called it, 'We've decided on internment because it's much more tasteful.'

Funeral suit also lacks mild concession to liberal déshabillé. Tom suggests this could be supplied by addition of jaunty Mutant Turtle baseball cap worn back to front.

Banish Tom from my bedroom (only temporarily – *so far*). Decide on my navy blue polyester suit which does not betray signs of exertion, emotion, etc. There was a time when if anyone had suggested I would ever wear navy blue polyester I would've bitten their head off and spat it over the horizon. But now I have succumbed to it, as no doubt I shall succumb in time to the elastic support stockings and the small, whiskery dog.

Unfortunately no clean underwear available so put on a pair of Tom's Homs. On me they have a curiously deflated look. Tom suggests I carry my nightie and spongebag in the vacant pouch. Fear he has delusions of grandeur.

Meditate mournfully on the fact that such an insignificant anatomical variation can cause so much heartache. Remember with affection microscopic form of life studied in Biology 'O' level which did not have to bother with underpants at all. O fortunate Amoeba! Spared the counsellings of *Relate*.

Tom takes me to the station, kisses me on the nose and warns me not to misbehave in Cambridge. Misbehaviour! What a good idea. Perhaps he is worried that I may run off with even younger man. After all, he's pushing thirty. Well we shall see. Aware whilst standing on platform that I have chosen wrong shoes, i.e. crippling ones but, encouraged by the thought that it never stopped Mrs Thatcher, I soldier on.

Train leaves Rusbridge on time but soon stops for hours in what was once flower-bedecked English meadow but is now uniform green prairie. Perhaps it would have been quicker by undernourished fourteenth-century pack horse after all.

Suddenly realise I have to give speech in four hours and have never in my life had interesting thought about either sport or TV. Pray that train has irrevocably broken down, but at that instant it lurches back to life. No pen or paper in bag. Lie back, close eyes and prepare to ransack brain and commit the resulting debris to memory.

forty-six

MOMENT OF MAXIMUM HORROR. Despite my assiduous avoidance of Cambridge Union during my three years at Newnham, find myself on front bench of The Chamber as guest speaker. Required to urge that This House Would Rather Slump in Front of the Telly Than Get Sweaty on the Sports Field. Sod's Law dictates that I must speak next to last, prolonging nervous ordeal of the imagination. Not sure whether to faint or have diarrhoea. Wish I was slumped in front of the telly. Brain maliciously informs me that I could have been, had I had the sense graciously to decline the invitation instead.

During contributions from floor, am distracted by delicious young man opposite who appears to unite the charms of Rudolf Valentino and Bugs Bunny. I give him meaningful glance and wonder if, afterwards, he will have the guts to fly to my University Arms Hotel room.

Struck by extreme youth of participants. So many eager young faces gathered together, radiant with intelligence! What a horrible sight. Odd. Recall that, in my day, the Union was the resort of adults, albeit asinine ones. Now it appears to have fallen into the hands of engaging children.

Realise the Union has not changed – 'tis I. Middle age has me in its grip, from navy blue polyester suit to mean, pinching shoes. All I need is British Airways cravat and I could pass for Tory MP of the hanging and flogging persuasion.

My turn to speak. Rise with audible creak of ancient sinews. Embark on speech, and wish, not for the first time, that I was The Beast of Bolsover. Though on train speech seemed brilliant, it has mysteriously lost its sparkle and become a catalogue of cliché and dreary innuendo. Company laughs however – generously, I feel. Debate is concluded with massive defeat for motion. This House Would Rather Get Sweaty on the Sports Field than Slump in Front of the Telly, apparently. Hypocrites! Or is it the callow inexperience of youth?

In taxi to hotel, recall that Tom and I once got sweaty in front of the telly. Feel that this act united the blessings of both endeavours. Ring Tom from hotel and am reassured that all is well at Cranford Gardens: Henry and Harriet not only still alive but fed, bathed and asleep.

'Your old man rang, though.'

'What!?!'

'I told him I was the lodger and I was babysitting while you addressed the Cambridge Union.'

'What did he say?'

'God help the Cambridge Union.'

Offer endearments and gratitude and ring off. Gratitude is so very tiring. Prostrate myself and await Morpheus.

Kept awake however by unpleasant reflections. Tracey could easily have been entrusted with the care of children till tomorrow, and the slipping of a few quid would avoid necessity for gratitude – and guilt.

Realise why life has been replaced, at the moment, by porridge. Feeling guilty towards Spouse a universal experience – nay, a wifely duty. But feeling guilty simultaneously towards quasi-secret lover something of an overdose.

Think, with affection, of the children. At least feelings of guilt towards them are soon blotted out by their ghastly behaviour towards me.

Suddenly recall there is a packet of crisps in handbag. Sit up and eat them. Am about to throw empty packet away when remember that Harriet would want me to take it home so she can keep it as a pet. I'm the one who'll have to feed it and clean its cage out, though.

Fragments of soggy crisps between teeth but bathroom two yards away and, besides, I am grown up and alone so can be as slobbish as I like. Snuggle down to enjoy rare treat – night alone. Brain maliciously informs me that had I not got involved with Tom, could have enjoyed whole year of such luxury whilst Spouse in u.s.a.

Irritated by presence in bed of five thousand crisp crumbs. Once more treat has turned into trial. Brain further irritates me by serving up unwanted proverb about necessity, having made one's bed, of lying on it. Wish brain was more like teeth. Would prefer to take it out every night and leave it in glass of water on bedside table. Fall asleep, and dream I am Prince Charles's bosom chum, and we are reading Shakespeare together.

forty-seven

MAIL ARRIVES. GRAB IT and retire to study whilst children breakfast amid debris of the Great LEGO and Plasticine Disaster. Open first letter.

'WATCHDOG DOORKNOB ALARM. . . . Just hang the electronic watchdog on the inside of your door. Set the sensitivity and relax. The alarm is activated by any slight touch of the doorknob. Should someone try to enter, an 85-decibel alarm will quickly change his mind. . . .'

Advertising blurb on back of Truprint envelope also promoting Cadbury's Twirl. Conjures up a bleak vignette of modern life: woman gazing at photographs and gobbling chocolate bars in locked room protected by 85-decibel alarm.

Scan mail in vain for letter from Spouse. Am invited instead to 'discover the unique presence of Tresor . . . . a perfume with a history, a memory. You know that when you wear it you won't be forgotten. . . .' Except by Spouses of the cold-blooded Caledonian persuasion, perhaps, basking on the sun-soaked campuses of the Midwest.

But lo! An envelope with real human handwriting falls out of the stack of soft-sell. Vaguely recognise handwriting though not sure whose. Black italic usually heralds communication from one or other of my old Newnham chums. Open envelope and find within erotic Indian carving and legend: *I love you* in – I now realise with flush of shame and alarm – *Tom's* handwriting.

So. He sends me billets-doux by post even though he's living with me. Eyes fill with tears but oh God, they're tears of pity. Luckily he went to work early today so will not witness them.

Rise briskly from desk and stride into kitchen where children are bickering over the last Weetabix. Attempt to divide it equally between them but it disintegrates and somehow most of it gets into Harriet's hair.

'Never mind,' grins Henry. 'Her hair's like Weetabix anyway.'

Harriet howls in indignation at this insult.

'Don't worry, darling. My hair's like Weetabix too.'

'No it SNOT! Your hair's LOVELY Mummy!'

'Look, look, hush: there's a Sindy token on the back of this packet.'

Rip token from empty packet and hand to the half-placated Harriet.

'Can we send away for one then?'

'Er no, we need to collect another . . . few tokens.'

Crumple up remaining bits of cardboard and throw into refuse bin, as Rusbridge does not yet offer facilities for recycling cardboard.

'No, Mummy! Don't throw it away! I want to keep it as a pet!'

'Look here, Harriet, I'm getting a bit tired of this. Some things just have to be thrown away because they're finished with.'

'Feel *sorry* for the rubbish. *Cruel* to throw it away!'

Harriet retrieves and cradles fragments of cardboard, now unpleasantly stained from their brief visit to the domestic Beyond. Cannot summon up energy for further argument, so acquiesce. Yes, she may take her pet cardboard to school. She may even take it to the vet when it gets a bit dog-eared for all I care.

'*Not* funny! Don't be *horrible*! *Laughing* at me!'

'Sorry. Never mind. Forget it. Get your coat. *Get your coat. Get your coat!* And your schoolbag. Your BAG! You NEED your blasted bag to put your bloody pet cardboard in!'

Harriet's reluctance to discard what is finished with particularly irritating to me, somehow. Such a scene would never have been allowed to develop in the good old Dark Ages. Spouse could have stopped it with a single quiver of *The Independent*.

Driving back from school run, stop at newsagent's and purchase Cadbury's Twirl. Mood lightens as we near Cranford Gardens. Will not think of Tom/Spouse dilemma.

Run indoors, upstairs, fling myself on bed and unwrap Twirl. Devour it, not as languorously as sultry siren in Flake advert, but nevertheless enjoying it to the hilt. Admire framed photographs of children on wall. The silence of photographs particularly charming.

Suddenly realise I am inhabiting vignette of modern life:

woman alone in room eating chocolate and looking at photos. But not bleak; in fact, pleasant. Perhaps I should send away for 85-decibel doorknob alarm after all.

forty-eight

STARE OUT OF STUDY window and notice single magpie on lawn. Feel irrational dread. Eat packet of peanuts. Irritated by irresponsibility of Government, allowing single magpies to fly about country causing alarm and despondency. They should be netted and submit to an introductory agency. The rest of us endure the discomforts of bonding; why should magpies escape?

Eat another packet of peanuts. Have developed tendency to secrete nuts in study, to minimise need for forays. Why?

'Would you like a cup of tea, darling?'

Tom sticks his head round door.

The frequency of these offers has not quite obliterated their charm. I do not really want a cup of tea, though. Tea has lost its savour since he insisted I stop having milk and sugar because they produce Bad Karma.

'No thanks. Not this time.'

'Who was that on the phone just now?'

Moment's incredulity.

So he didn't really want to offer me tea. He was on a spying mission. Jealous! The novelty of being an object of jealousy lasts fifteen seconds. Then outrage sets in.

'What the hell is it to you who it was?'

Aware that crisp dynamism of outrage marred by infelicitous syntax. Tom blushes.

'Hey! Relax! Keep your hair on!'

Keep your hair on, indeed. Silly youthful cliché. Fleetingly imagine self as bald and furious. Indeed have snapshots taken in late 1940s illustrating this phenomenon.

'You don't own me, you know.'

My turn for silly cliché – middle aged this time.

'I'm all too aware of that!'

Glare at each other, locked in mutual indignation. Only thirty seconds ago he was offering a cup of tea, darling. And they say a week in politics is a long time. Ha! They should try interpersonal relationships.

'Look –' embark on conciliatory gesture. However, load it with too much rhetorical weariness, at which he understandably baulks –

'Don't bother!' – and performs Exit and Slam. Con Brio.

Eat another packet of peanuts. Go to fridge and devour half a jar of gherkins and all the remaining horns and rinds of cheese. Burp morosely and malodorously.

Phone call was only from publisher Jeremy D'arcy enquiring if Bonkbuster nearing completion. Rashly promised to deliver MS, liberally adorned with bonks, by mid-July. Uneasily aware that if I am to introduce required ratio of literary licentiousness, I shall need all the childcare I can get. Wonder what time Henry and Harriet will emerge from TV room. Consume three Jaffa cakes and one Petit Filou.

'Well, Miss O'Dowd,' murmured Peveril, releasing the gleaming enamel hasps of his Prussian braces with a sharp metallic ping, 'since we seem to have exhausted the art of conversation, may I have the honour of the next prone polka?'

Puce O'Dowd's white freckled flesh rippled luxuriantly above her groaning whalebone, reminding Peveril of the almond and cinnamon puddings his nanny used to serve him in the sunlit nursery at Szch –

'Mummy! Snot fair! Henry says Bananaman is stupid!'

Henry exhibiting irritation, these days, with do-gooding superheroes. Well, aren't we all.

Children demand Monster Munches and Ribena. Acquiesce, nay, join them. Monster Munches explode in the mouth and coat the teeth with damp, cheese-flavoured tissue paper. Exquisite. Children demand marshmallows.

Acquiesce. After all, *marshmallow* does sound a bit like a meadow flower.

Glance out of window and observe single magpie perched on garden fence. Wish I had a slingshot.

Eat three digestive biscuits and a jar of olives to take away the taste of marshmallow. And to keep me going till lunch.

Although perhaps I should Skip Lunch and Save a Life – my own.

forty-nine

LAST YEAR'S FIRST OF June. . . . Attempt to cast mind back but succeed only in pulling neck muscles. Mind becoming as gross and inert as body. Too many biscuits, especially Bath Olivers topped with Himalayan peaks of taramosalata. Bath Olivers so expensive now, could form alternative currency. The hard ecu may go soft but the Bath Oliver will never crumble.

Last year's First of June . . . by then Spouse had announced his impending departure for U.S.A. and I was poised in a state of delicious expectation. As for the year before . . . ah well. That was the summer of falling in love. Or the Unbearable Brightness of Leering. How Tom's eyes shone! Now they alternate between canine reproach and sulky aversion.

Must try and cast my mind back, not merely for purposes of self-torment but also to assist in several passages of white-hot eroticism which I must insert in hitherto tepid and flaccid Bonkbuster. If Bonkbuster is to become Bankbuster must steel myself for endless episodes of transatlantic fin-de-siècle slap and tickle.

Puce O'Dowd rose from the lake, the water streaming off her translucent limbs like Sauce à la Esterhazy off a succulent morsel of Ukrainian snipe. Peveril felt a pang of homesickness. How he longed to smell his beloved Urals again! But the miasma of nostalgia evaporated at the appearance, in his dogwood thicket, of Puce's dripping paps and pert arriviste . . . what did she call it? – butt.

Hastily he extinguished his cigar, haunted by the memory of the unfortunate incident at the picnic at Brizbloč when he had inadvertently set fire to the Countess Irina Dabitoff's pubic hair. Peveril handed Puce a towel, and closed his eyes – partly out of chivalry, partly to obliterate the memory of that scandalous faux pas. Luckily his man Dmitri had had the presence of mind to make water upon the unfortunate Countess – something a gentleman could never have attempted. Perhaps the common people had their uses after all.

'Never mind the towel, honey,' came Puce's tormenting tones. 'Ah want you to pat me dry.'

The next instant a shrill shriek rent the sleepy Southern air. Puce sank to the ground, clutching her ankle.

'A spotted Tennessee swampsnake!' she sobbed hysterically. 'It done bit me on the foot!'

Peveril saw the speckled coils and in an instant he had despatched it with one deft lunge of his topaz tiepin. He flung the scaly corpse into the lake, and turned to his groaning companion.

'Never fear, Madam,' he assured her. 'I shall call my man Dmitri to get the poison out. He rejoices in a suck of considerable power.'

Puce only groaned.

With a dextrous fling Peveril covered the hapless nymph's nakedness with his regimental cloak, so that only the stricken foot protruded. With a whistle he summoned Dmitri who had been dozing with the horses in a nearby chestnut grove. Quietly he gave Dmitri his instructions, and the youth fell to his knees, licking his lips in a particularly gross manner.

'Don't you worry, sweet'eart,' he growled. 'I got a suck on me like a brook lamprey. Master'll tell you as much.' He bent, sucked, and spat the first mouthfull out all over Peveril's pigskin summer spats. 'There's nowt like a bit o'blood and venom before supper,' he affirmed, and returned to his task.

Peveril could not help observing that, as he bent, the youth's shirt was drawn out of his breeches and up his back, revealing what he believed was vulgarly known in Tbspsvili as plumber's bum.

Roused from my putrid passage by those last two fatal words. Feel seized by the ovaries and propelled out of my study – by the Goddess Aphrodite, no doubt. Pause briefly at foot of the stairs where soft snorts inform me children are safely asleep.

Televisual sounds lure me into sitting room. Tom sprawled on sofa in attitude of alluring abandon. Kneel before him – heavily, alas. Furniture shakes slightly. With shy greed of six-year-old unwrapping birthday present, unbuckle his belt.

'Hang on a minute,' he absently arrests my progress. 'I'm just watching *Thirtysomething*.'

fifty

Tom away for the weekend – visiting his friend Dog at the meditation, healing and organic rhubarb community at Llanwrchllgch-y-Bwlch. Strange, the Welsh reluctance to open their vowels. Feel more at home with Mama Mia, Casablanca and Ama-na-gowa. Though not aïoli, oie and Meursault – the French always go too far.

Wave goodbye with disturbing cocktail of relief and regret surging in breast. Tom gives me enigmatic look as if he is about to be killed in a road accident. Pray not, though increasingly worried about his van, held together these days only by pollution and corrosion; rather like Soviet Union.

Audrey Twill next door pops head over fence and asks if Henry and Harriet would like to come over as Henry could give Bernard a hand with the mowing and Harriet loves playing with the doilies, and that would give me a bit of time on my own wouldn't it? Audrey shoots me odd look. Not sure if sympathy or censure. Wonder what she expects me to do with my time to myself: fall to my knees and beg Juno's forgiveness?

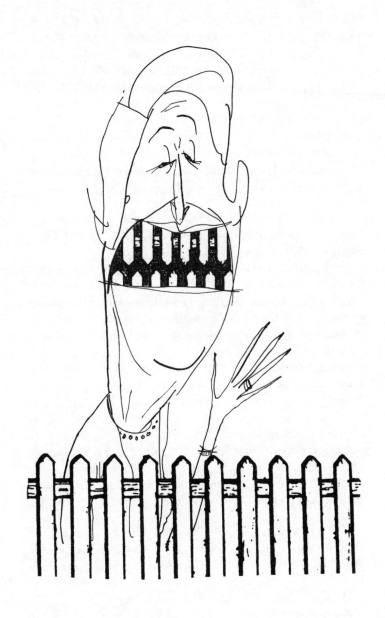

Prize children away from TV with bribery, blackmail, and threats of G.B.H., and deliver them, sulking palpably, next door. They cheer up at sight of Battenberg cake. Recall, walking up own path, that aforementioned cake was staple diet of Joe Orton and Kenneth Whossname, who killed him with a hammer. Wish Bernard Twill's mower was not electric, somehow. Though Harriet at least not involved in life-threatening activity. Cautiously confident that no-one ever died of doilies. Though knew a seaside landlady once who was getting dangerously close.

Sigh deeply. Though stalked by Websterian shadows, must address myself to Bonkbuster and rites of Venus.

'Oh, Count!' panted Puce O'Dowd, 'Oh, Lawd! You're so bold! Why, here, in the churchyard, of all places! Why, on mah Gran-pappy's tomb, to be sure!'

She lay helpless, all passion spent, on the slab of Mexican marble, her white limbs rudely tumbled in a flurry of pink satin, like an insect caught in the petals of a rose Peveril remembered seeing in the gardens at Count Battenberg's place on the Rhone, the Chateau d'Orton. And the name of the rose? Peveril turned his back to the lady, adjusted his dress, and wracked his brains.

Empress Josephine, that was it. Peveril recalled that, though the petals were a sumptuous pink, the scent was disappointing. But then, Peveril's experiences with women had all been a bit like that.

'I don't know about you, my dear, but I could murder some oie aïoli and a bottle of Meursault.'

'Lawdy, Count! You're such a picky eater! You're goin' to have to settle for Hominy Grits and a glass of Mint 'n' Pecan Cola.'

Peveril's gorge rose, but with the silent skill of caste and breeding, he swallowed it again. When in Rome. . . . Ah! If only he was.

Weekend endured without fatalities, though Harriet in tears at the discovery that a tree in the garden has died – the only one she could climb. Privately fear that Harriet's climbing it could have led to its demise.

'Snot fair! *Sad*! Make the tree *better*, Mummy!'

Murmur comforting platitudes about the death of trees not

the end, but leading to cricket bats, writing desks, dear little rocking chairs, and reams and reams of lovely drawing paper.

'Right!' says she, drying her eyes. 'I want a writing desk of it. And a rocking chair. And a rocking horse.'

And trustingly waits for me to expedite this at my earliest convenience, i.e. now.

Tom returns from his trip to the Celtic consonants bearing bushels of rhubarb, a carrot resembling Rudolf Nureyev in mid-pirouette, and a strange, round stone resembling Clive James in mid-sardonic squint. Nevertheless Tom is uncharacteristically sombre.

'Dog did my Tarot,' he reports gloomily, 'and I got the Three of Swords and the Tower Struck by Lightning.'

'What's that mean?'

'I'll tell you,' he promises menacingly, 'when the children have gone to bed.'

fifty-one

'IN THE TAROT,' PRONOUNCES Tom portentously, 'The Tower Struck by Lightning means that any project not securely founded on good feelings, will collapse. And The Three of Swords means separation. The end of a relationship.'

A short silence falls, during which my stomach rumbles and I feel an acute desire to eat a jar of olives.

'Er – would you like a cup of tea?'

Tom leaps to his feet.

'Typical! I try and get you to face up to things and all you can do is run away and put the kettle on.'

Suggest that putting kettle on and facing up to things not necessarily mutually exclusive.

'Sod the kettle!' cries Tom masterfully, blocking my way to the sink. 'Just listen, Dulcie. I'm going to be kicked out in a couple of weeks when the Lord and Master returns from the u.s.a. right?'

'Not – not necessarily.'

Voice falters and face twitches. Would not, I fear, inspire confidence as salesperson of used automobiles.

Tom grasps nettle unflinchingly. Cannot help admiring his guts – and being glad one of us has got some.

'You're never going to face up to him, are you? You're never going to have it out with him. You're just going to string me along and muddle through mess after horrible mess. You can't be straight with him or me because you're a total emotional coward, Dulcie. I'm sorry, but it's true.'

'I never said I wasn't a coward.'

Aware that my performance in this scene is far from distinguished. Tempted to sack the scriptwriter who seems to have given Tom all the good lines.

'Well, I've had it up to here.' Tom fails to indicate exact location up to where he has had it, but suspect Plimsoll line just above eyebrows. 'You are wonderful, yeah. I was crazy about you. I still could be crazy about you if I thought there was any future in it. But there isn't. Is there?'

Hold on tight to kitchen table and shake head dumbly. Outside, Mr Twill's lawnmower starts up in the silence. Wonder if Tom's aria of indignation was broadcast through open kitchen window.

'I think I'll go, then.' He picks up his bag, and runs his fingers through his hair.

'I'm sorry.' My voice has been replaced by Dalek croak. 'If it hadn't been for the children . . . it's so . . . you've given me the best two years of my life.'

Tom shoots me burning glare.

'It could have been a lot more.'

Cringe and gaze passionately at the kitchen floor, where observe enough food debris to feed Indian family for a week.

'I'll collect my stuff on Monday morning when the kids are at school. It'll be better if you're out. I'll leave my key on the hall table.'

Tears spring from my eyes, thank God. It's the least I can do. Other, truer, finer tears, course down his sleek young cheek. Then he goes. Front door slams, I swear, *hollowly*, living up to literary precedent. He has gone irrevocably I feel this time, leaving me with many magic memories and half a bushel of organic rhubarb.

Tears mysteriously dry up and heart uncurdles. Brain, going off on one of its eccentric sallies, informs me that though hitherto Addis Ababa was pronounced as such, recently certain reporters have started calling it Addis Abar-bar. Much as Peking was changed, overnight, to Beijing, without any of the general public being consulted. Wonder what my brain is up to.. Offering asinine distraction, or coded message about Mutability?

Go upstairs and gaze gratefully at sleeping children. *If it wasn't for the children.* . . . Kiss them, observing that they are never more charming than when asleep.

Reflect that Tom was much too good for me, and perhaps that is why a peculiar sensation of relief is stealing upwards from the soles of my feet.

Open all the windows, lean out and admire the midsummer night.

fifty-two

'MUMMY! ALTHOUGH YOU'VE GOT skinny hands I still love you.'

Touched by this filial devotion in the face of my over-whelming repulsion. Also glad I at least have skinny hands. The rest of me, alas, is coming to resemble a sea-cow. Am rapidly developing a tolerance, nay a longing, for the veil – or indeed any other garment that would reveal only skinny hands. Wonder if Spouse will return from the U.S.A. as a Born Again Muslim.

'Mummy! Where's Tom gone?'

'He's gone to help the people in Africa.'

'What? With Princess Anne?'

'I don't know. Perhaps.'

'Mummy! Why is the sky blue?'

All this before 7 a.m. on a Saturday. Forty-eight hours of solitary childcare to get through before I have an hour to myself again.

Not sure if Tom has offered his services to v.s.o. but he had mentioned it several times, as appropriate therapy for broken heart. Imagine the African night punctuated by the muffled sobs of relief workers in their tents. Should have given him his marching orders myself, really: spared him the awful responsibility. No guts, though. Completely pusillanimous. Only one thing more painful and messy than end of affair: family Christmas. Reflect that we are now halfway towards one, and shudder. I'm a real Noël Coward.

Cook large amount of fried bread for the children. Summon them from TV but am ignored. Eat fried bread myself, dipping it in HP sauce. Feel gratified but sick. Wonder if this moment of peace will last long enough for a bit of literary dalliance – the only sort, now, that I'll be able to indulge in. Grab pen and smooth out virgin paper bag.

Peveril arrived early for the tryst. But his heart was as heavy as the scent of the swamp jasmine which hung over the summerhouse in the late afternoon heat.

'Ah, Dmitri,' he sighed. 'This is a most disagreeable task for a gentleman. To inform a lady – or, in this case, Miss O'Dowd – that I must soon take my leave.'

'Her's a tasty enough little trollop,' observed Dmitri slyly, with an unpleasant smack of his proletarian lips. Peveril seized his silver tipped cane and brought it down with a smart swish upon the youth's ludicrously pronounced buttocks.

'You will not,' he hissed, 'insult any woman who is involved with me!'

Dmitri rubbed his posterior and Peveril a lewd wink.

'Fancy a quick thrash, then, guv?'

'Go! Wait beyond the sweet chestnut grove.'

Dmitri left, with a final provocative gesture which reminded Peveril of the hours he had spent in his hide at Yeltsinborg, observing the spotted Baltic wagtail.

He sighed, and strode up and down. In half an hour she would be here, with her flaunting corsage, cheap scent and wicked tongue. Peveril could not consort with her without a feeling of desecration. It was wonderful and yet sickening.

He pulled out and consulted his onyx and amethyst Fabergé fob-watch. A moment's hesitation, and he strode off towards the grove of sweet chestnuts. Perhaps he did fancy a quick thrash after all. Desecration was something for which Peveril had a robust appetite.

'Mummeeee! Where's our fried bread?'

'Sorry, darling. I've eaten it.'

'You bastard, Mummy!'

'Don't you dare call me that! Santa might be listening.'

'Santa's not real anyway,' Henry gives me wilful glare. Reward him with threatening look. Harriet panics.

'There is a Santa isn't there Mummy? He is real, isn't he? Mummy? *Please* say he's real!'

Recall that I once decided that midsummer was the right time to break the awful truth.

'Yes, darling, yes. Of course he's real.'

I don't know. I throw away the forbidden fruit, and am somehow still knee–deep in lies and desecration. And it's still only half past eight.

fifty-three

ENLIST MRS BODY'S HELP in cleaning house from top to bottom, though avert gaze from cupboard under stairs whence issues a strange stench suggestive of the charnel house.

'Mummeee! Can we make a banner saying *Welcome home Daddy*?'

'And hang it out in the road please Mum?'

'Er . . . well, make it first and we'll decide where to hang it later.'

Anxious not to trumpet forth in the street my domestic arrangements especially as Tom's van was till recently installed in road outside gate, like a quaint decaying Gothic lodge.

'Great! Mum, can we have a piece of paper twenty feet long?' *Bless them*, says Mrs Body, they're that excited.

Smile wanly and attempt to conceal own lack of excitement. Though residual anxiety persists as to whether I shall get away with it, am rapidly developing a strange indifference to almost everything. Perhaps I am turning to stone. Perhaps it's the rain. Try to remember details of Lot's wife. Was she wicked, and if so, in same mode as myself? Did she look back, or was that Eurydice?

Determined not to look back lest recent past rise up, like chimera, to engulf us. Do chimeras engulf? Or am I thinking of Vesuvius? Classical education runs away through my oolitic fissures. Have certainly blotted my copy-book *vis-à-vis* heaven, and though I have turned to limestone, fear I must forfeit my niche in the Abbey. Unless the Archbishop gets really modern and initiates Sluts' Corner.

'One last embrace, my dear,' sighed Peveril, surreptitiously glancing at his watch behind Puce O'Dowd's shuddering shoulder blades.

'Oh, Count!' she sobbed, with a melodramatic panache very far from the demure gravitas Peveril would have preferred her to exhibit, 'How can you do this to me? How, how, how?'

She tore her hair, bared her breast and beat it, and sunk her teeth deep into his tibia. Peveril bore the assault without a tremor: he had endured the tusks and fangs of wild boar in the forests at Kamikazy.

'Please accept my most heartfelt apologies, Madam,' he murmured, and summoned the hovering Dmitri with an elegant twitch of his right eyebrow. Dmitri prised the distraught girl from his master's carapace and carried her off, sobbing, to a waiting coach. Peveril adjusted his dress and stared moodily at his Jezebel cufflinks, then gazed beyond the Tennessee Boldwoods, eastward, beyond the mists of the Atlantic

coast, beyond the great sea itself, to the graceful birches, cool mosses, and almond porridges of his native land. Yeltsinborg! How he longed to plunge out of the sauna again, and roll amongst the frosty ferns.

By now, perchance, Charlotte would have tired of her treacherous assignation with the absurd Cherbagov. By now, surely, she would be crouching in rags by his gate, like Odysseus' dog, a pathetic figure. And as he strode once again across his threshold, her destiny would be in his hands. Would he find a modest place for her in a corner of his kitchens? Dash her from him in a fury of scalding pain? Or lead her tenderly back to her boudoir and bidet and bid her wash and dress for dinner?

Peveril did not know. But it was going to be interesting. At least, insofar as life ever was.

Depressed by the conviction that bonk-ratio still falling far short of publisher's desired objectives. Reconcile myself to torrid affair between Peveril and icy, perverse Englishwoman on transatlantic steamer. Punctuated of course by the odd playful appearance of Dmitri en déshabillé, as cabin cruiser.

Children produce large welcome banner on computer listing paper reinforced with Sellotape, card, Pritt stick and, I suspect, lipstick. Banner welcomes father home and offers beguiling representation of end of the world, with stars, moon, crazed princesses, Scud missiles, erupting volcanoes, and rampaging floods of baked beans. A kind of divine fusion of Nostradamus and David Icke.

Modest degree of apocalypse might quite usefully distract returning Spouse. Pray for plague of frogs, and double century by Viv Richards.

fifty-four

BOWLING ALONG THE BIRCH-LINED *track in his Porschke, Peveril's heart thundered beneath his lovat travelling cape. Any moment now he*

would glimpse the pale pinnacles of Yeltsinborg up ahead. Over on his right, the bronze dome of St Mikhail Ignatieff's twinkled above the treetops, and on his left, behind some ferns, was the turf roof of the bothy where the mad old hermit Pyotr lived with his pet wolf Spotr. Was Pyotr still alive? And what of Peveril's old nanny . . . he could not remember her name exactly but he was sure it began with an A.

A group of peasants were erecting hurdles around the covert of coppiced Cornus *where the gamekeeper Zoltan kept his prize Phrygian pheasants. The peasants, and possibly the pheasants, fell to their knees, crossing themselves and tugging their forelocks as he bowled past. Peveril raised a kid-gloved hand in a regal salute but shrank further back in his seat.*

Then Dmitri, seated aloft by the coachman, gave a coarse whistle as they passed Gudrun the young goatherd. Peveril noticed she had bosomed in his absence. He was glad to see his livestock doing well: he would summon her to his private apartments and ask her to serenade him on her pangolin.

But a finer, paler face flitted through the haunted corridors of his mind. Charlotte . . . had she come to her senses? Would he find her, crouched repentantly, at his gate? – Yes! There was a tumbled figure there – Peveril adjusted his monocle – but no. It was only a fleabitten old dog biting its arse. Peveril shuddered, and thanked heaven he had been born a member of Homo Sapiens. It was bad enough, in the course of his gentlemanly duties, occasionally to be called upon to bite other people's. . . .

Feel uninspired, but then, does the Muse ever hover over the Arrivals Lounge at Heathrow? Could lead to radar enigmas and even catastrophic air miss. Brief glance at monitor informs me Spouse's plane has landed. Put away Bonkbuster and visit Ladies. Apply lipstick, though without aesthetic intent. Survey result and blot off.

So. Spouse returns to a de-Thatchered land. But new ordeals await him – such as the awful spectacle of John Major in the Commons, struggling against nature to be nasty to Labour.

Wonder if Spouse will want a federal marriage, or will he be satisfied with a loose affiliation of sovereign persons? So much water has passed under the bridge, etc., that I fear its props may give way. Install myself at the barrier which restrains the horny-handed multitude awaiting the recently landed. Something Dantesque about it, I should think. Must read Dante one day and find out.

Large numbers of dazed Japanese arrive, rolling trolleys loaded with expensive matching luggage. Unnerved by this parade of Oriental chic, I hide my dog-eared, bald and possibly rabid handbag under my mac. The recently landed all look dreadfully ill and, in the case of Spouse, dreadfully ill-tempered.

For lo! He hoves into view, wearing a martyred air which suggests trolley-wheeling beneath his dignity. Remember similar reluctance with pushchairs. He has less hair than I remember, but then, I have got used to – but never mind. His glare intensifies, indicating that he has recognised me. Once we are face to face he bestows strange, raking glance suggestive of vet examining ropey old cow.

'Well, I must say,' he observes, 'you've certainly put on a bit of weight. You look just like your mother.'

Feel this is grounds for secession, setting up my own parliament, and establishing my own currency. Alas! A single currency is my destiny, and it is in Spouse's pocket.

'You don't look so bloody wonderful either.' Unfortunate and adolescent riposte – but that reference to my mother a cruel dig. She was twelve stone, for goodness' sake.

'Thank God the children aren't here,' sighs their devoted father, collapsing tragically into passenger seat. 'You realise that as far as I'm concerned it's three o'clock in the morning?'

Accusingly. As if International Time Zones, nay, the tendency of the earth to revolve around the sun, all my fault.

'As far as I'm concerned,' I snap, 'it's been three o'clock in the morning – *all year*!'

Ho hum. Journeys end in lovers' meeting.

fifty-five

ARRIVE HOME TO FIND front gate festooned with banner. Originally it said *Welcome Home Daddy* but heavy rain has translated it into Polish. Spouse spent journey from Heathrow alternately sleeping and complaining hysterically about lack of sleep. Children hurtle down front path and fasten themselves to his lower limbs like piranhas.

Mrs Body immediately sets about making a pot of the strongest tea – Assam – which she refers to as Assad or, occasionally, Saddam. No wonder it's fatal.

'There!' she exclaims, as Spouse collapses in kitchen chair. 'Lovely to be home again innit, eh?'

Spouse replies it will be, in a week.

'Daddy! Daddy have you got presents for us?'

Spouse evades the question and forbids further discussion on the subject until he has recovered.

'When? When? When can we mention presents again Daddy? And is it a Sindy Princess?'

'Is it a Space Station?'

Spouse goes pale and buries head in his hands, implying that any further contact with his progeny could send him reeling over the edge. Well, why not? I've been over the edge all year, I've been well down the abyss, mate. I've been clinging to the last thorn bush.

'Look, you two – go and play outside and leave Daddy in peace. He's tired.'

'Why's he tired? It's not even *our* bedtime.'

'He's come all the way from America and in America it's only five o'clock in the morning.'

'Why?'

'I think I must go to bed. Now,' moans Spouse, raising his head piteously from the table.

'Bless him! Just get that cup of tea down you first, Mr Domum. They don't have proper tea in America, my niece

Sharon told me. "It's like blinking dishwater, Aunty," she said.'

'I'll take it with me,' murmurs Spouse, and limps upstairs. Discreet flush half a minute later suggests the Saddam has gone down the lavatory. Hope it will not strip all the enamel off. Often muse that Mrs Body's occasional bouts of racism particularly ironic, since she and all her tribe must, from the regular transfusions of tarry Typhoo, be coal-black within from the tonsils down.

For next two days Spouse remains perpetually asleep, only making occasional forays downstairs to complain about the lack of Bath Olivers, Stilton and Dundee Cake and, on the other hand, iced water, air conditioning and swimming pools. Harriet, mystified, concludes that he is bewitched.

'Maybe, Mummy he's like Snow White – he's got to sleep forever until he's woken by love's first kiss! Go on Mummy! Go upstairs. Give him love's first kiss!'

More tempted to administer love's first kick.

Why the hell should he have the monopoly of tiredness? Own eyelids permanently at half-mast, these days. Hope for Dietrich effect but privately convinced iguana effect more likely. Crawl upstairs with light, aromatic cup of Darjeeling, plate of Bath Olivers and Stilton. He is awake, looking at the ceiling. Awake! Why not, therefore, downstairs and looking after the children, giving me a well-earned break? I've been on duty for almost a year, dammit, taking care of them single-handed. Well, almost single-handed.

Sit down on bed, compose features carefully into sympathetic smile, offer elegant snack, express hope that he is feeling better and wonder if he might find it possible to get up and supervise his offspring for the two hours before bedtime as he has not properly seen them for a year and I am absolutely exhausted.

Spouse fixes me with irritated glare. As usual, his tiredness is a tragic burden heroically borne, whilst mine is an irritating personal weakness.

'Ah well,' he sighs, sipping his Darjeeling with martyred smile, 'back to the world of pre-menstrual tension, eh?'

Much later, just as I am dropping off to sleep, realise with horrid qualm that I have not experienced pre-menstrual tension for absolutely ages.

fifty-six

SEIZE DIARY AND PERFORM menstrual mathematics. Two, four, six, eight: expiate. Diary taciturn on the subject. Pre-occupied instead with dentistry, birthdays of nieces, etc. Rack memory in vain. Diary usefully distracts however with minor disasters: Harriet's hearing test at local hospital, tomorrow, which had totally slipped my mind, and no doubt will again ere dusk.

'Harriet, you've got a hearing test tomorrow.'

'Eh?'

'What's wrong with her ears?' Spouse looks up accusingly, as if in his absence I have shamefully neglected his daughter's orifices – nay, allowed the wilderness to reclaim them, kites and crows to nest therein, etc.

'It's since that ear infection at Christmas. She's gone a bit deaf.'

'She seems perfectly all right to me.'

'Well that's because you're deaf, too.'

'What!?'

'There you are.'

Spend rest of day trying to remember what I read somewhere about the failure rate of the coil. Three per cent was it? Also legendary tales of babes born brandishing them like the infant Hercules strangling serpents.

Am suddenly aware, passing the chemist's, that there is a range of chic and tasteful pregnancy tests available. Would never dare buy one in Rusbridge, however. Would be sure to bump into Bernard Twill at chemist's counter in search of Audrey's *Anusol*. Will have to drive to Swindon.

Desperate for a doughnut in High Street. Purchase and devour whilst looking in shop windows to create illusion of privacy and minimise affront to the shade of my old head-mistress: *Gels must never eat in public or be seen with their hats orf, or frequent the lower part of the High Street, evah.*

I dunnit, please, Miss. I frequented the lower part of the High Street and here I am with sugar all down my chin. It seems I may be coming to a sticky end.

Recall, whilst purchasing organic beef, that a friend of mine once said the worst thing a woman could do would be to foist a cuckoo on her husband; pass off a sinister babe as his. Apart from the moral veto, practical obstacles overwhelm this other-wise seductive scenario. Since his return from U.S.A., nearest Spouse has come to amorous gesture is to pick a bit of Play-Doh out of my hair. Cannot recall last exercise of marital rights. Certainly Pre-War. Any outbreak of vamping on my part would be highly suspect act.

Harriet's ear test usefully interposes. We are ensconced in soundproof room with irritatingly cheerful and probably unpregnant woman. Harriet fitted with headphones and urged to put a counter in the cup every time she hears a beep. I am invited to hold the cup, and find this invitation rather patronising – or in my case, matronising. The sort of physio-therapy usually offered to those who are past it. If only I were.

Harriet's performance fitful, though I can hear every minut-est beep even without the headphones. But then, I am cursed with supernatural ears. I can hear most of what is happening in Oxfordshire, nay, in Colombey-les-Deux-Eglises. I can even hear what they will be saying in the future. Especially in Cranford Gardens, Rusbridge if this electronic barrage fails to jolt the errant hormones into action.

'You look well, Gudrun,' murmured Peveril, chucking the blush-ing goatherd under the chin. 'You have filled out nicely.'

'Nay sir! Nay!' the unfortunate girl burst out, flinging herself to her knees at her patron's feet. 'I must throw myself upon your mercy! I am with child!'

Peveril removed his pale gold kid smoking slippers from her drooling embrace, and sauntered peevishly to the window.

'In that case, my child,' he sneered, 'I have no further use for you. Let him who enjoyed you, provide for you.'

'Her hearing is within the normal range,' smiles the consultant. Are you reassured?' Forbear to inform her that it will take a lot more than that to reassure me, these days.

fifty-seven

'TELL US HOW YOU would choose to take the First Prize . . . . Rather than a cash lump sum, you may prefer £2,000 per month for life.' Always have same thought when reading this: if you chose £2,000 per month for life, and then lived rather inconveniently long, would the company send you a visitor along the lines of The Grim Reaper? The Great Consumer or The Dark Digester?

'. . . just sit back and enjoy the lifetime monthly income of £2,000 while you paint, sculpt, or write that great novel!' What a ghastly thought. Reference to That Great Novel a tasteless intrusion on private grief. Would prefer to enjoy £2,000 a month whilst sipping Baume de Venise in the bath, picking my nose and seeing if I could flick the bits as far as the ceiling.

'Claim up to three mystery gifts,' urges a card adorned with peas, silver and green, tumbling from open pods. Not engaged by this offer, though cannot resist temptation to *scratch off any three silver peas to reveal score.* (Twelve – equivalent of starred First.) Discard mystery gift card, however, as participation beneath dignity of anyone with a degree. Even a

Third. Do not like appearance of silver peas either. Suggests contamination by mercury.

This kind of activity always an evasion of painful duty. Usually The Next Chapter. Today, however, it's the purchase of a pregnancy testing kit – The Next Chapter with a vengeance. Select chemist in remote suburb of Rusbridge, recalled from old driving lesson days of yore. Take basket and serve myself with suncream, tights and sponge I do not need, in the hope that dim girl at till will not notice pregnancy test secreted thereunder. Or perhaps in some way notice it less.

Back home, hide pregnancy test kit in drawer where any woman of spirit would keep her lingerie, and I keep my *aertex coms*. Spouse unlikely to go fossicking about in my drawers, but all the same, slip fatal box inside sock as extra precaution. Nevertheless it seems to me that box is emitting electronic beeps like tagged offender on parole. Fear that Spouse may be enigmatically drawn to it by extra-terrestrial extra-marital vibes.

At 2 p.m., I hear him go upstairs. I pursue him into bedroom, heart in mouth (tastes vile). He opens another drawer and takes out cotton socks. Tears his own off.

'Bloody nylon rubbish,' he grumbles, though I have never bought him any but organic ones. 'Make your feet stink.'

'It's always better – I think – to get cotton or wool,' I suggest, with modest self-effacing tone, pretending I am on laundry-collecting mission.

'Must've been a present,' he growls. 'From a sadist.' Re-shod, he departs. Unnerved, I retrieve pregnancy test and smuggle it into my study. Slip it behind *The Reader's Digest Book of What To Do in an Emergency*. (Unhelpful in present crisis.)

Meet Spouse in hall. He is acquiring a curiously defenceless air – uncharacteristic and not at all becoming. He is, after all, about to receive a highly inconvenient Mystery Gift. ('I was gobsmacked.' – Mr D.D. of Rusbridge.)

'Fancy a cup of tea?' he asks. 'I'll do the school run today.'

What is this sinister accumulation of favours? Has he, too, a guilty secret? Is he about to trump my Mystery Gift with an Unrepeatable Offer? Has a sadistic sock-pedlar entered his life?

We sit down to Lapsang and crumpets, though I am too choked and tense to eat in his presence these days, preferring to gobble on the run like a free-range turkey.

'Tea was taken early because of Bad Light,' quips Spouse. Wish bad light was all I had to worry about. Would gladly spend rest of life in crepuscular soup if I could be relieved of present predicament.

'Well, how are things?' he suddenly looks directly into my eyes, without apparent reluctance, like a man newly emerged from a coma.

'I'm having awful trouble with my novel.'

'Stuck?'

'Mmmm. Just won't come. I sit there for hours twiddling my thumbs and . . . nothing.'

'Maybe you should try a hot bath and a bottle of gin! Ha, ha!'

The frightening thing about Spouse is that he's psychic, but the reassuring thing is, he's too thick to notice.

fifty-eight

URGE SPOUSE TO HAVE lie-in and promise to bring him breakfast in bed, etc., in order to get up early and privily conduct pregnancy test.

'What's all this tender solicitude?' he asks, understandably suspicious. 'How big's your overdraft?'

It's not the size of my overdraft I'm worried about: it's the size of my undercarriage. Explain I am enduring a rare philanthropic mood and recommend that he exploits it to the hilt. He acquiesces, still looking askance. Smile reassuringly despite inner turmoil. Know how John Major feels.

Rise early, retrieve hidden kit, pee deftly therein, secrete in study and leave to develop. Sip jasmine tea in delightfully – or perhaps ominously – still dawn kitchen and try to ignore frantic hammering of heart.

Peveril sighed – but literary endeavour hopeless. What did Peveril ever have to sigh about, smug bastard. Tempted to break new ground in romantic fiction and bestow upon dashing hero inconvenient pregnancy.

'Dash it, Dmitri,' sighed Peveril, massaging his enormous belly and burping discreetly, 'I've got heartburn again.'

'You put yer feet up and I'll get you a cup of tea, luv,' soothed Dmitri, 'and then we'll do our breathing exercises, shall we?'

Sure it will be positive. Odd use of the word. Medical profession only do it to confuse. 'I'm very sorry, Mr Jones, but it's positive: you've got Stoom-Kronkheit's Syndrome and I'm afraid that within two months your toenails will all have dropped off.' Negative is good news – would be in my case, anyway. Attempt to hum *Accentuate the Positive* but forget both words and tune.

Mentally consult friends. Alice brisk. 'No problem, Dulcie: tell him you're having a weekend in London and we'll get you a D.&C. – This is what we campaigned for, for decades, remember?'

Sorry, Alice. D.&C. out of the question. Would rather be turned out on wild night with shameful bundle containing curly and naïve baby – i.e. not Spouse's. His would be bald and venomous.

Mentally consult great heroines of the past. Cleopatra advises me to brazen it out. Elizabeth I recommends incarceration of Spouse. Mary Stuart (very sympathetic) suggests taking out a contract on him. Mary Tudor not available for comment owing to phantom pregnancy.

Consult those first enemies of the nuclear family and orthodox morality: the Romantic Poets. Byron startled at first, insists he never met me, then says he can't see what the fuss is all about: Spouse has his son and heir and in Venice I would be allowed my *Cicisbe* (historic precedent for toyboy) and no–one would turn a hair. Wordsworth shudders, grabs his rucksack, and runs from the room. Keats asks if I have told Tom. Shelley runs his fingers through his curly hair, calls for a vegan curry and – Gadzooks! – Shelley *is* Tom.

Consult statesmen of our own era. Major suspects my predicament may inconvenience me for some considerable period of time. Tebbit tells me to get on my bike. Only Cecil Parkinson really sympathetic. Realise now always under-estimated him.

Find myself abroad somewhere, possibly Transylvania, initially with Cecil Parkinson but he cycles off, leaving me ransacking chest of drawers containing photographs, desperately in search of a negative. Distracted by baby crying; go to crib, and find instead there, dressed in Mothercare babygro, large friendly Frog. Thought runs through head: *thank God it's a Frog. I can pass it off as Henry's latest pet.* Frog looks saucily up at me and says 'Where's that famous breakfast in bed you promised me, then?'

Frog turns into Spouse, though Prince would have been more welcome. Find I have dozed off in kitchen chair. It is 9.30 a.m. and my neck is permanently cricked. Apologise, leap up, feel faint, sit down again. Children run in demanding bread and jam. Spouse demands scrambled eggs. Uneasily aware that cupboard is bare and only available jam is that occupied by myself and only egg, my present facial adornment.

Tempted to run off and be sick but bathroom now myster-iously five miles away.

Shrug charmingly and pray for earthquake.

fifty-nine

IT's POSITIVE. NOT SO much the wages of sin – more the overdraft. Pregnant by recently-disappeared lover, unknown to recently-returned Spouse.

'Mummeee! Can I have a yoghurt?'

'Yes, darling.'

Though Spouse remote and unobservant, fear that fully-fledged baby would not escape his notice.

Assume this is Juno's revenge: claiming for Family Values what was by rights the rites of Venus. But knowing Venus she will effortlessly have her revenge. Cannot understand how Christianity ever managed to supplant Graeco-Roman polytheism, since everyday life bears convincing evidence of supernatural squabbling, shit-stirring and point-scoring.

Meanwhile this hapless handmaid of the gods casts wildly about herself upon the dusty road from Thebes. Perhaps will set next Bonkbuster in Ancient Greece. Then could engineer erotic episodes not just amongst Homo Sapiens but many-headed monsters. But which politicians of the present day could translate convincingly into Athenian garb? Though Kinnock may hector, I cannot see Major as Achilles.

Prefer Napoleonic era. Better frocks. Suddenly recall film by Rohmer called *Die Marquise von O*, set in Napoleonic wars, in which innocent young widow becomes mysteriously pregnant whilst in drugged stupor. Wonder if I could convincingly conjure up tale of drugged stupor: *I just dropped off in the park and when I woke up it was Tuesday and my dress was a bit tumbled about.*

At the thought of breaking it to Spouse, a lead cricket ball forms in my stomach. Offer him cup of decaffeinated Earl Grey. Do not wish to over-stimulate him. Wish I had some of Friar Lawrence's Kip for Nine Months and then Wake Refreshed pills. But what then? *Look what the man from Red Star brought, darling?*

Is this the moment? Lead cricket ball swells to football size. Henry absent, camping (only literally, I trust) with Julian; Harriet gobbling her yoghurt and glued to her video of *The Secret Garden*. Do not like title *The Secret Garden*. Sounds too illicitly fecund.

Will not tell him now. Better to wait till Harriet in bed. Or she may run in at the very moment when Spouse places outraged hands on my neck. Unless he merely raises an eyebrow and strolls out of my life, accompanied by his bank account.

'Mummee! I feel sick!'

'Don't be silly. You're never sick. It's probably just a burp.' Harriet burps loudly ('You *are* clever, Mummy!') and withdraws.

Comforted by the thought that I need not tell Spouse till 8.30, or even 10 p.m. Could enjoy, till then, five hours of serene domestic routine, i.e. serve up braised lamb without acknowledging presence on head of blazing coals. Terrified at necessity of throwing myself on Spouse's mercy as convinced he must have had it removed as a child, along with his tonsils.

Harriet is eventually immobilised, complaining of headache. Give her two teaspoons of Calpol. ('Ugh! Not that orange flavour, Mummy! Why can't they have salt and vinegar or smoky bacon?') Go downstairs and enter kitchen. Spouse is stationary behind *The Independent*. Clear throat. Enough lead in stomach now to re-roof York Minster. . . . Will not tell him now. Will wash up first.

Never has washing up, or indeed life itself, seemed more futile. Dirty water gurgles down drain with sadistic chuckle. Have never envied small fragments of dead lamb before. But off they go, with a carefree whoosh! and never a backward glance.

Spouse still concealed behind *The Independent*. It's now or never. Lead in stomach mysteriously becomes molten and pours down the backs of my legs.

'Whilst you were away I got involved with somebody.'

Silence and stillness. Has he died behind there?

'Mummee! I'm going to be –'

Loud sounds from hall suggestive of Harriet first being sick, then falling downstairs. Rush out to hall and find her at bottom of stairs, bruised and befouled. Carry her upstairs, cuddle her, place her in bath, and realise with ghastly pang that I had been meaning to throw away that yoghurt for weeks. And then, all of a sudden, another, less ghastly pang convinces me absolutely that I am not pregnant any more.

sixty

'So WHAT WAS ALL that about your bit on the side?'

Spouse wearing satirical grin. Tempted to wipe it off by announcing affair with Daley Thompson, but refrain.

'What?'

'Your bit on the side. You were just about to tell me all about it when Harriet was sick.'

'Oh that. That was a hearing test. As administered to husbands behind newspapers by wives uncertain of their survival.'

Bend down and fiddle with sandal strap, thus hiding face in skirt. Skirt smells of sour milk. Sandal strap breaks.

'No toyboy then? How disappointing. What a very dull life you lead, Dulcie.'

Bite tongue. Wish I was pregnant after all. With alien quads. That'd wipe the sardonic smile off his face.

'What about you, then? No transatlantic peccadilloes? Didn't any of those corn-fed freshwomen tickle your fancy? Or don't you have a fancy any more? Is it beneath your dignity?'

Spouse sighs, and folds up *The Independent*.

'What I really fancy,' he says with a yawn, 'is a slug of Old Bushmills.'

Reluctantly abandon prospect of marriage-shaking row and instead set glass of amber fluid before my lord and master. Prefer Aqua Libra myself, although herbaceous border has so far failed to break out all over my diaphragm.

Moment of danger having past, and further cohabitation seeming unavoidable, guilt evaporates leaving good old reliable anger. Spouse still smiling superciliously at me. Time to give him both barrels, the bastard.

'We're going to Weymouth for a week on Saturday,' I inform him sweetly. 'And when we get back it's Aunt Elspeth.'

'Oh Christ!'

Anguish floods the Spouseian countenance. Best moment for several weeks.

Spouse having failed to produce the letter from mother excusing him for games, we all depart for Weymouth on schedule. Usual scrupulous division of labour: I pack, make sandwiches, clear out fridge, cancel milk, ask Audrey to water garden, immobilise children in back of car with Walkmen, etc., etc., whilst Spouse moans and flaps. Ah, but he does it so divinely.

He also claims severe headache – futile attempt to escape holiday – so I must drive. After his first disparaging remark about my judgement, I round on him with dripping fangs and threaten to run off with the aspirins at the next service station leaving him with the children, holiday, etc. Thereafter my exemplary prudence about overtaking (only if road clear for two miles in each direction) only provokes the occasional martyred sigh.

Arrive in Weymouth. Seafront sparkling, large numbers of the fat and the old promenading thereon, bless 'em. Thanks to my sterling research we are installed at charming Georgian hotel with car park, instant access to beach, no roads to cross, etc., etc. Spouse admires eighteenth century stairwell but complains about soft bed. Inform him he is in any case to sleep on the floor.

We congregate in sitting room to wait for dinner, along with pearly cluster of maiden ladies, or perhaps widows (o happy state) who admire Harriet's curls. TV is on, showing teen movie of the Grease genre. Talk to maiden ladies about hairbrushes, all trying to ignore teenage couple on TV in back of car caught up in split condom situation. Harriet and Henry gawp at screen despite my efforts to interest them in jigsaw.

Idea flashes through head to market jigsaw depicting erotic scene in Bangkok brothel: jig-a-jig saw.

'Well,' says Spouse as gong sounds, 'that's given me an appetite.' Not sure for what.

We go into supper, though a couple of the pearly widows linger with intent by the TV, hoping for further depravity.

Supper excellent, served by mine host, a striking Viking whose manner suggests he would rather rape and pillage us than convey to our table steaming plates of home-made tomato soup. (Excellent, though children whine for Heinz.) Whine for Heinz, another brilliant advertising gambit, I am wasted on pulp fiction, wasted.

After supper walk on beach, trip and severely sprain ankle.

sixty-one

A SPRAINED ANKLE IN Weymouth sounds promisingly Austen-esque. But alas, no dashing Captain available to catch me – defence cuts, probably. Instead of being caught by dashing Captain, am rebuked by damning Spouse.

'Why do you never look where you're going?'

'Well, yes, why don't I?' I cry sardonically between gasps of pain. 'Why didn't I look where I was going in 1978?' (Year the Domum marriage was perpetrated.) Spouse frowns, looks flummoxed.

'What happened in 1978?'

Nothing my Lord.

Spouse sulks continuously thereafter because I have been inconsiderate enough to sprain my ankle on arrival. All the charging about, fetching things, nipping to the shops, etc., normally executed by me thus falls to his lot. By the third day he pronounces himself tragically exhausted. Ignore this lament, because am myself up to the neck in Panavision Technicolour sulk about his lack of sympathy.

Plenty of sympathy from Harriet, though. She makes a tender-hearted nurse. Indeed from what one reads about the N.H.S., it may soon be commonplace for a whole ward to be in the care of a six-year-old girl equipped only with bucket and spade. Sit on beach for hours reading old newspaper. Harriet, looking over my shoulder, pounces on cartoon about sperm bank.

'Mummee!' she roars, 'what's a Spam bank?'

'Don't shout, darling, you're disturbing everybody.'

'But what is it? What is a Spam bank tell me!'

'It's where they sell Spam.'

'Can I have a Spam sandwich? Can I please? I haven't had any Spam for ages.'

'Nor have I and I'm not making a fuss. You can have crisps.'

She grabs the 20p and bounces off on sound young ankles.

An enormously fat man flubbers past.

'There,' observes Spouse, 'goes a potential Spam donor.'

Days pass in a twinkling maritime haze. Reassured, though repelled, by the presence of so many people even fatter than me. Oxfam should film their next famine appeal on Weymouth beach. Fattest thing in our party is my ankle which has swelled up to resemble a Zeppelin.

Host at Hotel informs me they have a resident Physiotherapist who might be able to treat it. Physiotherapist, sturdy Scotsman with soothing manner, recommends massage and I am conducted to treatment room, handfuls of gel slapped on leg and massaged from top of thigh to tip of toe. Scotsman complains that massage has got a bad name these days, but that if I enjoy it I should recommend it to my husband. Suppress a smile at the thought of Spouse willingly submitting to anything pleasurable.

Back on beach, ankle improved but am haunted by the sense that something wonderful, dynamic and sexy has gone out of my life. At first I assume it to be poor Tom, but later realise it is in fact the West Indies Cricket Team. Alas, shall I never see Viv Richards bat again? Viva Viv. Or should that be vivat? It seems my wonderful, dynamic, sexy Latin has all gone too.

'How's the work been going?' enquires Spouse, perhaps recalling dimly that a couple of thousand are due on delivery of manuscript of Bonkbuster.

'Pretty pathetic. Can't seem to get enough bodice-ripping in.'

'Yes, well, you always were an awful old prude. You know your trouble? Not enough adventures when young.'

Refrain from comment. Wonder if I shall manage any more adventures ere I die. Perhaps I should leave Spouse and children on Weymouth beach, marooned amidst the acres of charbroiled British Spam, and hot-foot it to new life as, say, physiotherapist to West Indies team. Imagine: someone is actually paid to caress the sinews of Curtly Ambrose.

Fall into light doze beneath Spouse's panama hat, and have ambrosial dream in which I live in exquisite hut on palm-fringed beach, often rise to the challenge of Malcolm Marshall's bouncers, and am regularly stroked to the boundary by the elegant and demure Carl Hooper.

Rudely awoken by bucket of cold water thrown over me by rampant son and heir. Perhaps just as well.

sixty-two

ACCUMULATION OF DISASTERS. RETURN from holiday means that nourishment of family no longer in capable hands of Weymouth hotel cook. Ankle still weak, children bored, and Aunt Elspeth rolling menacingly southwards. Spouse, going through the post, announces:

'You've been sent an anonymous postcard saying *Remember: Nostradamus predicted it all.*' Seize postcard and frown in specious puzzlement, though I instantly recognise Tom's Liberal's Italic. Scrutinise postmark and am relieved to find *Vienna* – i.e. not too dangerously far south or east, but nevertheless reassuringly remote from Rusbridge.

'What do you suppose it was that Nostradamus predicted?' enquires Spouse. 'And who is this lunatic anyway?'

'It's Saskia's handwriting. She's into Biorhythms, why not Nostradamus?'

Annoying to have to lie long after extra-marital relations have been broken off. Like hangover without intoxication.

Recall that Nostradamus predicted dark shadow would fall across earth in early 1990s. Extraordinary that he could have foreseen so clearly arrival of Spouse's Aunt.

Frenzied preparations take all day: organic oatcakes purchased in bulk and stacked in pantry like perilous limestone pinnacle: sixty denier porridge, Wright's Coal Tar Soap ('It stinks, Mummy!'), Meditations of Thomas à Kempis on bedside table (polished with beeswax), mothballs in wardrobe and lavender bags in guests' drawer form basis of aged Aunt's life-support system. Haunted by sense I have forgotten something, and sure enough:

'You have put the hot-water bottle in my bed, haven't you, dear?'

Had forgot her fear of death by damp sheets. One would have thought whole of Northern Hemisphere adequately aired by end of August, but nevertheless, smilingly indulge her. She watches my struggle with old rubber hot-water bottle, a sceptical expression on her pursed lips.

'Ah, the old stone hot-water bottles were the thing, you know. They lasted for ever.'

Like the old stone aunts. Remark that aunt in visibly radiant health, and receive stern riposte.

'Ah but my piles, dear, are quite agonising, I'm afraid.'

'Mummy what are piles?' asks Harriet, detecting the indelicate with accuracy of heat-seeking missile.

'They're like grapes,' cries Henry, 'hanging out of your bum, and when you fart they sort of rattle!'

'Go to your room!' I snap, forestalling infantile request for recital by aged Aunt. 'Now! Or I shall tell your father!'

Children depart blowing raspberries in unison. Apologise.

'That's all right. I know how difficult this year must have

been for you, Dulcie. You look quite worn out. Thank goodness their Father's home again.'

Return of Spouse evidently implies restoration of Discipline, Totalitarian Terror, Censorship, etc., so desirable in the nurture of young children.

'Here's a little something for you – I thought it might make your life a bit easier.'

Aunt hands me enormous parcel. Unpack with delighted smile stapled to lips. Strange device revealed: resembles hand-held rocket launcher. For a moment suppose I am to point it at children at first sign of unrest. Then realise it is Soda Stream. Had one once, but it was decommissioned and given away to Mrs Body for her White Elephant stall.

'I've noticed you spend a fortune on that Perrier water, dear. Now that's a bit silly, don't you think? When with this, you can fill anything you like with fizzy little bubbles. Nothing need ever be flat and boring any more, you see?'

Express gratitude, and gaily observe that aged Aunt may have saved my marriage. High moral disapproval leaps into her face. Am reminded of old saying that a joke cannot be introduced into a Scottish understanding without a surgical operation. Wonder where Spouse is loitering, unfairly leaving entire effort of small talk to me. Recall that during last visit of aunt he invented bowel ailment and spent whole hours in the lavatory with Dornford Yates.

Aunt wonders if it would be convenient for her to stay an extra week.

sixty-three

Aunt Elspeth pads after me from room to room, insisting that there must be something she could do to help. 'Yes: stop talking,' springs to mind, though not to lips. Offer ironing but, alas, she must decline. The static plays havoc with her perm. Could she not, she suggests, with Calvinist frisson, clear out my drawers instead? What impertinence! Gently refuse, warning that there are things in my drawers from which even I avert my gaze. Aunt looks disappointed. No doubt these were the things she was most looking forward to inspecting – and holding against me for ever.

As I cook, she hovers by my elbow, jamming the BBC's news with a prolonged lament over the change of librarian at Kirkwhinnie. Decent old librarian apparently ousted by coup whilst at his dacha at Carnoustie. Offer Elspeth carrots to scrub. Alas, she has recently developed an allergy thereto. 'Just like my poor Ian. He had only to see a carrot, dear, and he'd be up all night.'

Mention of husband reminds me of Spouse, who has gone to ground during his aunt's visit, pretending to write important paper about Matthew Hopkins, Witchfinder General, who purged Essex of eccentric old women in the 1640s.

Suggest Aunt might like to summon Spouse to his table-laying duties but she would not disturb him for the world, insists on doing it herself whilst regaling me with horrid tales of her grand-daughters' recent injuries.

Become aware that I do not want lamb chop, or indeed anything much except silence.

Spouse enters kitchen accompanied by flickering halo. What is this? The aura of sanctity, projected by worshipping aunt? No. Cranial stab reminds me that heavenly flicker is ever the prelude to my migraine.

Children rush in: 'Ugh, not Lamb! YUK! I'm a vegetarian! Mummy Mummy what are bollocks? Mummy we found a place on the map called Pee Town NO WE DIDN'T Shut up Henry Give it me Mummy he's got it tell him not to WAAAAAA!'

Retire immediately to darkened room. Children follow. 'Mummy, can we have Hula Hoops instead of Lamb?'

'NO! Now get out or I shall be sick!'

Spouse appears and banishes children to kitchen.

'What's brought this on, then?'

'I'm exhausted,' I croak. 'I haven't had a moment to myself for a whole year, if you remember. I'm spent, I've had it up to here. And I want a baby.'

At the word *baby*, Spouse gasps and staggers backwards, mysteriously pressing his hands protectively over his jacket pockets.

'Have a rest,' he croons in most soothing tone he has used since 1973 when I fell off the bike on the way downhill into Norwich and my hip swelled up so much, I couldn't get my jeans off. (Fatal impediment to dirty weekend.) 'Have a nice rest, I'll make sure you're not disturbed, take it easy.'

Migraine soon lifts, thanks to modern pharmacopoeia. Arms and legs also lift, indeed, float right off and come to rest on the ceiling, but what of that? At last have moment to myself. Peace. Rest. Meditation. Wish I could think of something to meditate about.

A wasp flies in. Summon arms and legs back off ceiling, get up and reach for paperback. Wasp pauses on windowsill and cleans its antennae with admirable thoroughness. Somehow I cannot kill it, now I have watched it washing itself. Do not feel same compunction about Spouse, however. Attempt to steer wasp through window with paperback Proust but it clings to book. Finally throw out book, wasp and all.

Regain blessed horizontality, and wonder what I want from life. Not really a baby, I suspect. As often at moments of extreme stress, I realise what I really want is Herefordshire.

'Half-timbered houses,' I moan to Spouse. 'Half-timbered cows. On my own. For two weeks.'

'*Two weeks?*' he explodes, pale with outrage.

'No, you're right: three. And I'll finish my book.' Spouse splutters helplessly. 'Well, it's that or a baby.' Spouse instantly rediscovers backbone.

'Done.'

Feel I should have made it four weeks in Barbados, but never mind.

sixty-four

ON MY OWN IN the Welsh borders. Three weeks' voluntary solitude. Children left in care of Spouse, assisted by Mrs Body who announced her intention of giving the place 'a good going-over' in my absence. Wish she would do the same for Spouse, though fear it is too late for mere redecoration, and only renovation grant would restore him to original grandeur.

Have brought Tom's old love letters with me. Re-read them with only transient pang, and deposit in recycling skip. Pointless to keep them as they are a hostage to fortune and, besides, I cannot help being irritated by his inability to spell *definitely*. A spineless word, in any case. I shall avoid it in future. Not that I have used any words at all for days, except to waitresses and shopkeepers. Cobwebs festoon my larynx. I am getting Hostage Throat.

Question: if there were a General Election tomorrow, which party leader would I dream about? Drift off to sleep and dream of Clare Short, who has more balls than the whole pack of them. Awake with cramp. Though this farmhouse is picturesque, the bed is a spongy divan. Woo Morpheus with plans for radio programme called 'Desert Island Discos' in which one is invited to reveal which eight historical hunks one would most like to boogie with. Halfway through a jitterbug with Stormin' Norman I awake to find myself pinioned in the maw of the divan. Fear I may have slipped my Desert Island Disc.

Tactful autumnal mornings tip-toe into room at reasonable hour, unlike midsummer dawns which burst in shrieking with hammer at 4 a.m. Lie in bed, gaze out of window at Hereford cattle. One enthusiastic heifer seems to be pestering the bull, rather like schoolgirl asking for Pavarotti's autograph. Suddenly the bull mounts her, has his way, and four seconds later returns to grazing. Heifer looks astonished. Well, if she thought that was nasty, brutish and short, she should try a tanked-up public schoolboy.

Strange to lie becalmed in luxurious silence instead of being wrenched awake by the Babel tongues of my children. Lip quivers at thought of my babes. Fear I am suffering maternal deprivation – from the other end.

Farmhouse breakfast not till 9 a.m. at my request. Farmer no doubt rises at 5 a.m. to be milked by the Bank Manager. Lie and stare at ceiling and attempt profound thought. Brain instead observes that once upon a time there were only two kinds of bog-paper: IZAL and BRONCO. Attempt anagram therefrom, but cannot even conjure up Aztec deity.

What shall I do today? Linger o'er battlements and tumuli? Haunt damp old bookshops complete with forlorn ting-a-ling of doorbell? Dissolve into brown study in decaying orchard, swatting the last numb wasps? (There is a Keatsian languor about that last phrase which I feel angurs well for completion of Bonkbuster – object of present furlough.) *Languor, augurs, furlough* – Good Lord! When too much alone one's words go strange in one's head, like Arabic.

'O Solitude! Where are the charms / That sages have seen in thy face?' as Cowper remarked, who lived alone, and went mad. Human happiness surely depends on satisfactory balance between society and solitude. Oh, and TV. Aware with a flick of remote control switch (standard issue in olde British farmhouses) I could be invaded by Breakfast TV.

Admire reunion of John MacCarthy and Jill Morrell. Richly satisfying; like late Shakespearian comedy or Odyssey. Perhaps this is why it grips nation. Or, more likely, entire population hypnotised because all the women fancy him, and all the men fancy her.

How swiftly, in solitude, does one's sensibility coarsen! Why, I confess to having stuck a bogie on the underside of my bed last night, rather than shiver the two yards to my Kleenex. Shame propels me from my divan.

After several hours in Ludlow, I ring home two days before

schedule, desperate to hear the innocent lispings of my babes. Pray that Harriet's voice will not break with filial longing.

'Oh God, it's Mummy,' she says, sounding older and more irritable than I had remembered. 'Can you ring back later? Only we're watching Count Duckula and it's ace and fab.'

Wander off wanly, in search of Last Tango in Weobley.

sixty-five

RUGBY WORLD CUP: SPOUSE turns to stone in front of TV. Resembles statue of Abraham Lincoln in Washington, only less animated. Harriet stares at box and asks Why are all those men so fat, Mummy? All Blacks perform the Haka – supposed to terrify the opposition, but pretty tame compared to Harriet's tantrums.

At half-time, Spouse recalls epigram that soccer is a gentleman's game played by hooligans, whereas rugby is a hooligan's game played by gentlemen. Perhaps the world is after all divided into hooligans and gentlemen, united only in their dependence on the motor car, in which hooligans joyride and gentlemen kerb crawl.

Suppressing my secret preference for hooligans, I collect the post and receive letter from old friend who recently moved to Glasgow. Though a tall and imposing fellow, he was assailed whilst walking peacefully in the street by three pubescent urchins who roared: 'Arkin wha yeer yer dick aed!' ('I know what you are, you're a dickhead.') Perhaps hooligans not so attractive after all. Unless of course they were three of Glasgow's gentlemen.

Phone rings: it is Lydia Rainge-Roughver. 'Air hellair Dulcie! Hau augh yuargh? Flairshing? Just rang to make sure you dain't forget that there's an Apen Day at the school next Fridaigh.' The School, needless to say, is Crippetts, where

Emma Rainge-Roughver is doing so orfleh well even theough frenkly she's an apsloot dumbauh. 'I dain't neigh if Harriet's still happeh at Rusbridge Primry but she's so orfleh bright and at *Crippetts* they're tairrebleh good at mewsick 'n' ahse.'

This assault opens up old wounds. Had acquiesced when Spouse insisted on Henry's going private, justified by supposed density of son and heir's skull and necessity of small classes, etc. Nevertheless have felt vaguely guilty about it ever since. Last dregs of socialism perhaps. Despite my heartfelt faith in the state system, have recently begun to resent the way Spouse doesn't mention that Harriet might benefit from private education. Don't want her to have it, but don't want Spouse not to want her to have it just because she's a girl. Sigh hopelessly, promise Lydia I will present myself at the *Crippetts* next Friday just to have a look and then immobilise myself in hot bath.

In fact, have noticed with sense of foreboding that Harriet's class at Rusbridge Primary now a writhing thirty-five. Seeing them all trying to take their coats off in cloakroom recently reminded me of scenes from Rugby World Cup: what I believe is known as a maul collapsing into a ruck. Is she underachieving? I ponder. Well, it runs in the family. There were times when my father fondly believed I was going to end up in the Washington embassy, whereas I have ended up in a bath near Swindon under a peeling ceiling.

At least Bonkbuster is completed and despatched. Am waiting with baited ballpoints for Jeremy D'arcy's reaction, and even more urgently, part two of my advance. The only advances I'm likely to receive, these days. Still I've run my bath and I must lie in it. Who was it who expired in the bath? Socrates? Did they have baths then? The hot tap definitely scalding. Must ask Spouse to adjust what Mrs Body refers to as the Emotion heater.

Don't know what to do with myself in the bath now I'm not allowed to examine my breasts. That man Acheson who looks like a sad Spanish aristocrat from a Buñuel film told us we mustn't, any more. Instead we are to be constantly vigilant.

Take a furtive peep but can hardly see breasts at all, let alone lumps. Be alert for anything unusual such as a pucker. My dear Mr Acheson, I am all pucker from head to foot, these days. Indeed most of the West Samoan front row have finer bosoms than I.

After bath, enter sitting room where whole family is under-achieving in the flickering glare of the TV: Harriet with Sindies, Henry with comics, Spouse with rigor mortis.

'I'm going to see *Crippetts* next Friday,' I announce portentously.

'Who?' asks Spouse, without shifting his gaze from the screen where several gentlemen covered in mud are apparently biting one another's bums. Obscurely saddened by the thought that Harriet might, if privatised, cease to be a hooli-gan and instead covet horses and skiing. And how long would it be before I failed to understand a single word she said?

Collapse exhausted into chair and feel that the joys of under-achieving have been seriously under-estimated.

sixty-six

HARRIET RETURNS FROM SCHOOL slightly flushed and with lewd glint in eye.

'Peter Harris showed us his paeony today. In the playground.'

'*What?*'

'I held him so he couldn't move and Gabrielle pulled his trousers down and we saw his paeony. And Gabrielle wants to come to tea tomorrow.'

'You mustn't do that sort of thing, Harriet. It's naughty.'

'But he told us to! Don't shout at me Mummy you horrible poo-poo!'

Palm itches but recall Penelope Leach's advice to leave the

room at such moments. Stalk out with attempt at haughty disdain, but cardigan pocket catches on door-handle.

Later, whilst Harriet is watching children's TV, leaf through my Shakespeare in search of title for Bonkbuster. Undergraduate inscription on flyleaf going brown with age: my name and college in youthful script, aping handwriting of most admired don (who later blotted his copybook by goosing me whilst I was having a gander at some ancient MSS). He was a PhD: Doctor of Philandry.

Speaking of ancient MSS, perhaps I should get Alice and Saskia a copy of Germaine Greer's book on the menopause. But no, they are bound to have memorised every word already. Better idea: give it to Spouse as malicious Christmas present.

Lydia Rainge-Roughver rings to ask what I thought of *Crippetts* School Open Day. Realise with flash of horror that I entirely forgot to go, and hastily invent bilious attack. Lydia sympathetic, though we both know that bilious attacks are no longer available in the modern world. Now it's all allergies and post-traumatic stress syndrome. Lydia insists I must go and inspect *Crippetts* on my own, much bettah anyway, Emma's teachah Andreah Willoughby will show me rind, she's an apsloot sweetie. Listlessly acquiesce.

Later, leafing through what's his name – Shakespeare – wonder if my increasing forgetfulness could be symptom of pre-menopausal stress syndrome. Sort of P.M.T. writ large.

Fail to find title for Bonkbuster, though am briefly very taken with *O! O! O! (Titus Andronicus,* Act IV, Sc.II.)

Next day, forget that Gabrielle is coming to tea. Only thing in fridge: jug of sour milk, and half lb sliced ham, forgotten since last week. Examine ham: it is developing disturbing mother-of-pearl quality. Replace doubtfully in fridge and fall back on old standby.

'Gabrielle, would you like a jam sandwich?'

'Donlikejam.'

'Peanut butter?'

'Donlikepeanu'bu'uh.'

'Marmite?'

'Donlikemarmi.'

'Well, how about a stuffed tortoise with ladybird sauce?'

'Mummy!' Harriet furious. Nothing surreal permitted when friends come to tea.

'I like 'am.'

Gabrielle evidently saw me hesitating over the food archive. Reluctantly re-open fridge. Jug of milk performs somersault and drenches mother-of-pearl ham with stinking gouts of curds and whey. Rinse ham under tap and offer to Gabrielle who scoffs the lot.

Clean fridge out – with Harriet's approval since it gives fleeting impression of a proper Mummy.

Henry arrives home, dropped off after football. Asks if he may learn the trumpet. Gabrielle, fortified by her ham, casts him lascivious glance. Trust son and heir's paeony will remain tastefully secluded till bedtime.

Doorbell rings – further harassment, though one hopes not sexual. Though who knows what services may be available in a fully privatised realm. Good heavens! It is Alice, looking tragic and carrying – I notice with qualm – enormous suitcase.

'Saskia's left me!' she cries, 'for Lavinia! – *Lavinia*!' Express outrage, though alas have forgotten who Lavinia is. Except the one in *Titus Andronicus*. And I shall have forgotten who she is too by 10 p.m. *O! O! O!*

sixty-seven

ALICE SO RAVAGED BY grief at Saskia's elopement with Lavinia, she cannot remember the names of my children, and addresses Henry and Harriet – when absolutely unavoidable – as Harry and Henrietta. Harriet smirks uneasily, sidles up to me, and asks if she can whisper something.

'Whispering is not polite,' I intone, though not with absolute conviction. Recall several occasions when I was grateful that Harriet had the sense to whisper things that would have been catastrophic aloud.

'It's not the transfer of affection *per se* that's so upsetting,' Alice laments into her fourth Barley Cup. 'I mean one can accept that, one does not after all possess one's partner; intellectual freedom implies sexual and emotional freedom of course – but oh God! It's the deceit I can't bear, Dulcie!'

Express sympathy but wince inwardly. Hope Spouse has deceived me plenty of times in the past decade, but fear his habitual lethargy disinclines him to temptation. Not fair, really. Moral superiority should be striven for, not slide effortlessly into the laps of the lazy.

Feel purple passage stirring uneasily within, but now Bonkbuster is complete, have nothing to unload it into. Have not yet received verdict on rewritten MS from Jeremy D'arcy. Desperate for part two of the advance, and am halfway through delicious daydream about spending spree in Bath when I become aware that Alice has posed me a question and is awaiting a reply. Hesitate – sagely rather than vacantly, I hope – and the gallant Harriet leaps into the void.

'I've got a boyfriend,' she informs Alice proudly, 'and his name is Peter Harris.'

'How ghastly,' shudders Alice. She has never cultivated any kind of child-friendly patter: sees herself as heroically uncompromising. Harriet, of course, bursts into tears. Alice, not to be outdone in histrionics, joins her.

Henry gets up from his LEGO and marches out with face like thunder. Male inability to deal with strong emotion has evidently set in early. Wonder if I might be suffering from it myself. Have often thought I may have a few extra male chromosones, although I have not bleached my moustache since 1972 (and even then it was a political gesture: would rather resemble Lloyd George than Stalin).

Spouse puts his head round door and informs me that his

cousin Alistair has got tickets for some rugby match or other and he plans to take Henry off there for the weekend.

'We'll be out of your hair,' he adds placatingly, though I know that the secret agenda is that Alice will be out of his. Still, there is something curiously touching about Spouse's harmless urge to slope off for an extra-marital ruck. Encourage the trip with the effusive generosity of deep guilt. Though the thought of weekend alone with Alice and Harriet not alluring.

On the Saturday morning, letter arrives from Jeremy D'arcy telling me Bonkbuster is 'brilliant'. Pleased, though aware that nowadays *brilliant* has come to mean *mediocre*. Part two of the advance is 'on its way' – i.e. still slumbering in the dark depths of publisher's bank account.

Alice and Harriet locked in mutual irritation, since both wish to monopolise me. I am also irritated as I would rather like to monopolise myself. Half-heartedly suggest trip to place specialising in rare breeds of domestic fowl.

'Will there be chicks?' screams Harriet in an agony of anticipation, and repeats the scream every ten minutes during entire car journey (one hour and twenty four and a half minutes). Alice spends journey confiding further details of Saskia's perfidy, all of which I would have preferred not to hear.

Rare breeds of fowl extremely diverting, thank God: some looking like Dolly Parton, some like Billy Connolly. Observe that many cockerels seem to have the carriage of Michael Heseltine.

'Yes, and it's always the cockerel who comes to the netting to greet us, you notice,' remarks Alice sourly, disappointed by absence of feminist fowls. 'The wretched hens don't get a look-in.'

Most of the hens seem rather contented to me, but dare not say so. Wonder what life would be like if I had to share Spouse with several other wives, and conclude – alarmingly, perhaps – that it would be infinitely improved.

sixty-eight

UNUSUAL COMMUNICATION FROM MILKMAN: Christmas advertising blurbs. One offering 'The 1992 Dairy Diary'. Always had trouble with that, since a child. Same problems with A Life of Brain. Probably due to degeneration of brian cells. (*A Life of Brain* – biography of Spouse.)

Dairy Diary apparently offers 192 pages of information, including Household Emergencies and Recipes From Around Britain. (*Household Emergencies* – biography of self.) Recoil at thought of Rothiemurchus Collops of Venison, recalling glutinous experience at Kirkwhinnie at the culinary mercy of Aunt Elspeth. Besides, would rather not consume creatures with velvet antlers and long eyelashes.

Also recoil at the thought of yet more Recipes from Britain when I have not yet properly mastered the boiling of an egg. Mine emerge with cloudy polyps of escaped egg white clinging to their cracks, like Barbara Cartland in white fur stole.

'Mummeee! 'M'ungry!' Harriet appears, roaring. Recoil anew at thought of having to provide snack for offspring, let alone for lovesick vegan Alice, still loitering in spare room. Can I get away with vegetarian curry – again?

Harriet runs to my desk and grabs one of the milkman's blurbs.

'Caw! I wanna Chomp! No, a Twirl! No, a Boost!'

Henry appears in the doorway, alert to the possibility of chocolate.

'Can I have a Lion bar, Mum?'

Always had trouble with that, too, as in: *he felt an urgent trembling in his lions*.

'Mum mum can we can we???'

Resist advert's exhortation to Say It With Chocolates. Unless one could say Shut Up and Sod Off.

Go to kitchen and equip children with organic crisps and tell them to help themselves to bananas afterwards. They run off crunching.

'Stand still while you're eating!'

Ignored as usual, Luckily Alice not here to purse lips. She is enjoying one of the perks of the childless: a lie in. We encourage these.

Post arrives with *New Internationalist*. Whole issue devoted to food. Extraordinary account of Chinese Market offering mouthwatering array of beetles, wasps, lizards, raccoons, and dogs. 'A breed similar to Staffordshire bull terriers.' The biter bit, evidently. Chinese have a way with tofu – one of Alice's staples. 'Cook it in soup with a little salt-dried fish head and pork knuckle.' Not quite vegan enough, even for me.

As usual perusing *New Internationalist* leads to intense liberal shame and horror. Unremitting toil of banana workers in Philippines: health risks to them of pesticides, etc. Hurtle to kitchen, snatch bananas from hands of my children and hurl into bin. Offer organic carrots instead. 'Ugh no they're *hairy!*' Reluctantly issue strict ration of Jaffa cakes.

Return to *N.I.* and am horrified by working conditions in sugar cane plantations. Deforestation, destruction of habitats and protein-rich wildlife: workers now starving. 'His eyes mist over as he remembers how delicious armadillo used to taste.' And all to satisfy depraved Western craving for sweetness.

Run to kitchen but alas, the Jaffa cakes have been devoured. Alice has come down like a damp mist, looking tragic in Spouse's dressing gown which she must have filched from the bathroom. Usurping the monstrous apparatus of patriarchy, perhaps.

Agree instantly to children's demand to watch Captain Planet and explain to Alice that it's ecologically O.K. But she is not listening. Her eyes glitter strangely. Perhaps she has pre-tofu low blood sugar.

'I had a dream about you, Dulcie,' she says, restlessly fingering her tin of Barley Cup. 'I don't think you've ever realised – '

Spouse enters, recognises his dressing gown and gives it pitying look. Then turns urgently to me.

'Is it true that if you can't touch your nose with your eyes closed, you've got a brain tumour?'

Feel an urgent trembling in my lions, and suspect I am falling between the tips of two icebergs. Experience violent desire for Mars bar, but attempt to stifle it on ecological, socio-political and humanitarian grounds. Also because of its association with the god of war. Not completely convinced that armadillo would provide same degree of oral gratification. But, if Rusbridge Co-op can rise to the challenge, would be more than willing to try.

sixty-nine

'LOVED IT, LOVED IT: you are brilliant, honestly.'

Publisher speak with forked tongue. Translation: *complete load of twaddle, you are a talentless prat, but we'll never get the advance back so let's grin and bear it.*

'Oh no, Jeremy. I'm all too aware of its faults.'

'No, really, it's wonderful, but – '

BUT???

' – but this Gorbachev thing is beginning to look a bit dated, er, so do you mind if we give Cherbagov thick grey hair? And make him more a sort of big ugly bear of a man? Who likes his vodka and dives into the Volga to sober up? A bit more of a – er – barnstormer?'

Sigh, and concur. It's now no longer enough to be bald and dynamic with a brilliant gaze. One must get pissed and dive into rivers and have hair, apparently.

Ah, the inconveniences of democracy. The tendency of the many-headed multitude to get bored, to shift their restless appetites to the next big thing.

Longing, as usual, for benign Green tyranny, I enter the bathroom, to find Spouse examining his hands by fluorescent light.

'My hands are mottled,' he whispers urgently. 'What's that a sign of?'

'Too much time on them,' I snap. 'And if all you're doing in here is admiring your hands, push off!'

Spouse recognises the urgency of my gaze and evacuates the facilities in the nick of time. Damned vegan curries. I blame the sultanas.

Alice has left the latest copy of *Resurgence* beside the loo. I leaf through it, hoping for a life-transforming small ad. 'Shamanic suppliers: drums, rattles, feather items, medicine bags, shields, tapes, herbs. . . .'

Would like to become a medicine woman, but fear I could not afford the kit.

'Mummee!'

'Wait a minute! I'm on the loo!'

'Wanna poo now! Quick! I'm holding my bum shut!'

Fly to door, admit daughter, enthrone her and stand well back. What whole family needs is steak and chips followed by Spotted Dick and custard. The old fashioned sort of Spotted Dick, groaning with cholesterol. Struggle to suppress my sudden lust for suet, though tactful eviction of Alice an urgent necessity.

As I am wiping Harriet's bum, my eye falls on another *Resurgence* small ad: ARE YOU DYNAMIC, CREATIVE AND ENTHUSIASTIC WITH LONG TERM IDEAS AND COMMITMENT? Shudder and realise that perhaps I have got something to be grateful for after all.

Spouse's turn to shepherd children through Saturday. He takes them off to see *Honey I Shrunk the Kids*, leaving me, in theory, a peaceful afternoon in which to dream up my next Bonkbuster. New contract desperately needed, as overdraft is rising menacingly and threatens to burst its Bank.

Front door slams, alas: Alice returns from Green Light Food to Go bearing Hummus, Pesto, Halva, Tofu and other Balkan

resorts. My salivary ducts twang anew with longing for Spotted Dick.

'Dulcie,' she says, fixing me with meaningful stare, 'you and I must Talk. I don't think you're aware of just how liberating you would find it if you really surrendered to Voice Dialogue. It's a Transformational Tool, you know.'

Sidle furtively towards study, apologising for need to work till four o'clock, when I will meet her in kitchen for tea or even Hedgerow Infusion and surrender to her Transformational Tool.

In study, thrust aside mountain of bills and prepare to draft outline of new book. Heroine will not be limp Sloane this time, but prole whizz-kid, dynamic, creative and enthusiastic with long-term ideas and commitment. I hate her already. And her leading man will be based on one whose star is rising. Prepare to let my imagination play lasciviously over the Shadow Cabinet in alphabetical order. Though perhaps it would be better to save Gordon Brown till last.

This beguiling prospect interrupted by sudden arrival of Spouse who grimly informs me they had to come home early because Harriet Had an Accident.

Oh well. At least I am spared Tea with Transformational Tool.

seventy

WHISPERS AT MIDNIGHT. SPOUSE tossing uneasily on rank pillows and threatening to start smoking again.

'She's got to go.'

Alas, Alice has not yet disappeared through the looking glass, despite spending hours in front of it muttering darkly about forty winters besieging her brow. She has not departed for Wonderland, either, but is still with us, gluten-free muesli and all.

I sigh. What a wonderful thing a sigh is: a satisfying minor chord of concern and impotence. Feels nice too. Must be all that oxygen. Do another one. Not a chord: a cadence like the breaking of a wave. Or the turning of a page. Feels delicious. Do another one. Whoops! Feel faint, even though I am lying down. Mustn't overdo it. Must remember my forty winters.

Forty winters! Stifle a sigh at the onset of another dark season. Heard radio programme the other day about people who get depressed in winter – a condition called SAD. They have to sit under lamps until April, like vulnerable convolvuli. I thought feeling low in winter was the human condition, but never mind.

Agree that Alice must go. Ah, but how? Aware she is my friend rather than Spouse's and it is therefore my responsibility to engineer painless eviction. Could bribe children to be even more nauseating than usual – but perhaps not. God knows they've been doing their best.

Very agitated over rise of Neo Nazism in Germany, indeed in obscure parts of Rusbridge. Saw bald youth last week sporting Rudolf Hess T-shirt. At least, assume it was Rudolf Hess. Could only see the *Hess*, but doubt if it commemorated Dame Myra.

Next morning, opportunity presents itself for multi-cultural education. Whilst I am admiring pin-up of Jeremy Guscott, Harriet exclaims:

'I wish I was a browny.'

'You musn't say *browny*, darling, it's not polite. You should say Afro-Caribbean or Indian, perhaps, depending – but never mind, you're quite right, you're a good girl to admire people from other nations; they're often cleverer and kinder than we are – the way they live is better for the planet and their music and stuff is, well – lovely, really.' Harriet stares, evidently gobsmacked.

'No, Mummy, I meant I want to be a Brownie, but you can't be one till you're seven, and they meet on Tuesday nights, and it's not fair, and I want a uniform.'

'Ah,' remarks Alice, 'a little would-be brownshirt, I suspect.'

Rather than engage in a dialectic about militarism, I embark on a fantasy about Gordon Brown.

'Mum,' Henry looks up from his crypto-militaristic comic, 'can we have some chocolate brownies? Can you make some?'

'Sorry, darling. There's not a single nut in the house.'

'Well done,' smiles Alice grimly. 'An attempt at domestic enslavement neatly resisted.'

Experience unusual desire to bake a cake.

How to evict Alice? Invent visit from Great Aunt? Engineer burst water pipe above spare bed? Introduce Vita Sackville-West look-alike who will whisk her off to Sapphic Symposium? Decide on Great Aunt, and corner Alice at her muesli. With a flash of intuition, however, she pre-empts me.

'Don't you think, Dulcie, that one of the most *sinister* things, nowadays, is the way defenceless refugees are being hounded out, all over Europe? . . . Oh, by the way, I don't want to be a burden to you, so –' – light at end of tunnel? – 'I've decided I ought to pay you some rent. So here's two hundred quid.' Oncoming train.

Graciously attempt to resist rent. After all, it will imply rights. Alice insists, however. Pocket two hundred quid with sinking feeling. Feel my liberalism has become mysteriously slippery.

Retire to room and fall into brown study – nearest a kind-hearted person like me can get to black thoughts.

seventy-one

RECEIVE POSTCARD OFFERING ME free holiday in Spain in the interests of *Promoting Europe – Europe Unité*. Throw in bin. Also receive thank you note from charity bearing news that my measly £20 has saved several children's lives. Gratified, but suspicious lest aforementioned lives were actually saved by covert U.S. arms deal.

Reflect soberly thereon whilst washing milk bottles. Place milk bottles upside down to drain and notice that in this position they tweet like alarm call of blackbird. Ah me, nothing is what it seems in this treacherous world.

Sun comes out, at which spirits rise. But realise all too soon that sun has revealed thick dust on all horizontal surfaces. Feel dust has had a bad press. It is, after all, organic: evidence of biodegrading. Tempted to write something in dust on sideboard but cannot think of anything pithy enough to fit between candlesticks.

Meditate on Spouse's ultimatum: Alice must be out by Christmas Or Else. Or Else what? Fear he is on the verge of announcing Either She Goes or I Go and I am in danger of replying Fair Enough. Though curious by-product of Alice's prolonged sojourn: Spouse, hitherto alien oppressor, is evolving into fellow-conspirator. Must conjure up chimera of visit by great aunt. Or perhaps – even more effective – Norman Tebbit.

Sidle menacingly towards sofa on which Alice is innocently engrossed in novel by Storm Jameson. Open mouth to deliver regretful eviction notice but at critical moment phone rings. It is Saskia. Alice goes pale and dithers but is eventually urged towards receiver.

Withdraw tactfully to attic where I can eavesdrop through floorboards. Alas, Alice is terse, even gnomic. Saskia evidently delivering epic apology. Look round attic for distracting relics or perhaps hitherto unperceived Rembrandt but find only empty cardboard box which once held camping gas lamp.

'Mummee! Where are you?'

'In the attic.'

'Oh goodee!' Thunder of tiny feet on stairs. 'Poo! It pongs up here!'

169

Reassure, though privately convinced that something has died behind water tank.

Harriet fossicks in prehistoric debris whilst my eye loiters over camping gas-lamp box where manufacturers have praised their product in six languages. 'Powerful portable lamp' becomes in Italian 'lampada potente' and in German 'Unabhängige Leistungsfähige Lampe'. Tempted to indulge in xenophobic generalisations, but refrain. Great relief to find that, in Arabic, lamp becomes couple of discreet cusps and a mote or two of dust.

Somehow reminded of Norman Tebbit's observation that nobody likes to be governed by people who don't speak one's own lingo. Hence Welsh Parliament long overdue? Not to mention Brummie.

'Mummee! I've found treasure!'

Harriet produces battered purse but am obliged to inform her that it contains only lire. Recall charm of visiting Italy as a penniless student and discovering that I was mistress of tens of thousands. 'Penniless' – ah, how poignantly that illustrates the deep embedded socio-cultural whossname of one's own currency. They may impose their wretched tinfoil ecu on us but I shall spend nought but pennies until my dying day. And what of the literary tradition? *Said the pieman to Simple Simon, Show me first your ecu.* . . .

O what is the point of Europe if its infinite variety is to be replaced by identikit ecus and featureless supermercados to spend them in? Suddenly recall the farthing with its dear little brown wren. Eyes fill with Tebbitian tears – if such a thing exists.

Alice comes up to attic beaming and informs us that tomorrow she will depart for Santiago da Compostela where Saskia awaits. Greet this news with unfeigned joy. Though cannot help wishing the reconciliaton could take place somewhere less glamorous such as Swindon or Romford.

Harriet finds faded photo of her father aged eighteen months and pores over it.

'Ah!' she croons. 'wasn't I sweet!'

Do not disabuse her as convinced that mistaken nostalgia is the only firm intellectual basis from which to face the twenty-first century.